Surely *she* wasn't the new night sister?

A man who didn't much mind what he wore, Ben could yet appreciate style in others, and this lady had that in abundance. But she was younger than he'd expected. Pretty, too, in a fragile sort of way. Angelic, if you liked that type of woman, but he didn't. The job called for maturity, and, after the last night sister, he certainly didn't want any romantically inclined blondes!

Dear Reader

Caroline Anderson's PERFECT HERO has a shock in store, while Dr Laura Haley is determined to pull Dr Ben Durell out of his refuge in Marion Lennox's THE HEALING HEART. We welcome back Sonia Deane, who tackles the thorny question of doctor/patient integrity, while TOMORROW IS ANOTHER DAY by Hazel Fisher explores the recovery of two people who have been badly hurt in the past. Enjoy!

The Editor

Hazel Fisher was a late entrant into nursing and was briefly a general nursing student before deciding on psychiatry. She worked as a mental nurse for several years before writing full-time.

Having lived in East Sussex all her life, she admits that most of her plots come when she's doing the household chores! She enjoys writing medical romances as they provide much needed escapism—for her as well as the readers!

Recent titles by the same author:

CAROLINE'S CONQUEST
LUCY'S CHALLENGE

TOMORROW IS ANOTHER DAY

BY
HAZEL FISHER

MILLS & BOON LIMITED
ETON HOUSE   18–24 PARADISE ROAD
RICHMOND   SURREY   TW9 1SR

First published in Great Britain 1992
by Mills & Boon Limited

© Hazel Fisher 1992

Australian copyright 1992
Philippine copyright 1992
This edition 1992

ISBN 0 263 77886 X

Set in 10 on 11 pt Linotron Times
03-9210-54881

Typeset in Great Britain by Centracet, Cambridge
Made and printed in Great Britain

PROLOGUE

'GOODNIGHT, Doctor!'

Ben Moran gravely acknowledged the night porter, before making his slow, painful way to his car.

Rain, which had been threatening all day, now came down steadily and looked set for what remained of the night. Or morning, as Ben supposed it must be now.

He glanced back at the dimmed lights of the Easterwood Clinic, the rain soaking almost unnoticed into his jacket. When a patient's life was at stake, time just slipped by, hours and minutes gone forever. But at least Sophie Clary was safe now—until the next attempt. He had known Sophie a long time and had developed a certain cynicism where that family was concerned. It was a bad trait in a psychiatrist and he would have to watch himself.

Wearily, he tried to push back the lock of hair which persisted in falling over one eye, but the damp hair resisted his attempts and settled back in exactly the same place, giving him a raffish, piratical air. The blackness of his hair and eyes and the olive skin served to reinforce this effect—one of the reasons he was known behind his back as 'Ben the Buccaneer'.

His mouth twisting in a wry smile at the thought, Ben set the coupé smoothly in motion and headed out into the December darkness. His bed would be waiting. So, too, would Louise—if she was home at all.

A shower, hot coffee, a comfortable bed and several hours of deep, refreshing sleep, that was what the doctor ordered for himself. Somehow he doubted he would be that lucky.

* * *

With hands that were not quite steady, Jenny Fraser opened the white envelope. Recognising the handwriting as that of her ex-fiancé, she had carried the envelope around with her for most of the shift, strangely reluctant to open it. Yet words couldn't hurt her, nothing he said could hurt her now.

She was being a coward. A foolish coward, at that. Then the noise of the busy acute psychiatric ward faded into the background as she stared down at the newspaper cutting which was all the envelope contained. Just that. He had not even sent a letter, a few lines apologising, excusing himself, wishing her well for the future. There was nothing—save the cutting from the local paper announcing that a marriage had taken place.

'Sister?'

'Yes?' Jenny answered automatically, one half of her mind still on the announcement. How could he? How could *they*?

'Can I sit with you, Sister?' Let me,' the patient went on, and Jenny dragged her stunned mind back to the present, to the busy ward, to the patient standing in front of her desk in the tiny office. Yes, the patients came first. What did it matter if Sister's heart was broken?

Donna, the patient, was so wrapped up in her own problems that she probably failed to notice Sister Fraser's pallor, the shock in Sister's large grey eyes, the usually cheery voice that faltered for a moment.

Then Sister Jenny Fraser pulled herself together. So, Lloyd was a worm, a creep, a snake in the grass. What did it matter? She ought to think herself lucky that she had found that out *before* they married!

'We'll both sit in the dayroom, Donna. Tea should be along soon,' she said, her usual smile back in her voice and her eyes. Yes, a nice cup of tea, that was what they both needed.

Shepherding the girl out of the office and being careful to lock the door behind her, Jenny made her way to the dayroom. Her smile hid her broken heart, her shattered life—hid the fact that the man to whom she had still been engaged as recently as last month had chosen this cruel way to tell her of his marriage to someone else.

CHAPTER ONE

JENNY FRASER got out of her car, an ancient Mini, pausing briefly to admire the imposing Georgian Façade of the Easterwood Clinic. Even to her inexpert eyes, it looked the real thing, not some twentieth-century fake, a house pretending to be something it wasn't, just as she was pretending: a nurse with a shattered life masquerading as a calm, capable nursing sister.

At least no one could spot the masquerade from her appearance, Jenny assured herself, her eyes shadowing. Then, taking herself severely in hand, she locked the car and approached the open front doors of the clinic for her first spell of duty, a week on days before she took over as Night Sister at the renowned psychiatric clinic on the Sussex coast.

Knowing she looked her best gave her the confidence she sorely needed. Her suit wasn't new but its style was timeless, and the soft lavender-blue suited her fair colouring admirably. She only hoped Dr Moran would approve. No one had actually said anything, but she had gained the impression that the head of the clinic was *very* hard to please. Well, so was she, and, if the treatments at the clinic didn't come up to her own high standards, she would have something to say to him!

Jenny's lips curved into a smile as she walked briskly up the steps. For better or worse, here she was, ready to take on Dr Ben Moran and the whole world if need be.

The reception area of the clinic was both imposing and elegant, evidently the great hall in days gone by, though Jenny wasn't sure how that fitted in with its

Georgian exterior. A lofty, high-ceilinged room, it had partly wood-panelled walls with a number of intricate wood carvings à la Grinling Gibbons. The reception desk looked modern, but it was in a dark oak to fit in with its surroundings. There were a number of chintz-covered settees and armchairs scattered about, and at the far end of the hall Jenny saw a long table and wooden benches, like the 'settles' of Shakespeare's day.

For a moment, she thought she had wandered into the land of Alice. Then she caught the eye of the smiling receptionist.

'You're looking bemused, Sister!' the girl said, when Jenny introduced herself. 'Everyone does. We have everything here from Shakespearian through to modern times. Collector-mania, I call it!'

'I'm inclined to agree with you,' Jenny murmured, though she had to admit that the different periods blended in well together. Nothing looked out of place, not even the modern water-colour hanging on the wall behind the reception desk. And when Dr Moran's middle-aged secretary floated down the stairs, clad in a long, flowing print skirt and a ruffled white blouse reminiscent of Edwardian times, Jenny was able to greet her without surprise.

'Good morning, Sister Fraser. Welcome to the Easterwood!' The secretary, Babs Richardson, proved to be a brisk, no-nonsense woman with a motherly air, and Jenny took to her straight away.

'If you would like to follow me, I'll see you don't lose your way,' the secretary went on. 'Call me Babs, by the way. We try to be friendly here. As you know, the acute psychiatric suite is on the first floor, and down here we have Reception and a small ward for the older patients. Don't call them geriatrics, for heaven's sake! They're quite active, lively people when they're well. I'm over in Admin, which is the first cottage in the grounds, the one you can see from the drive. We eat over that way as well, in the second cottage. Gets us away from work.'

Jenny found it wasn't necessary to do more than murmur, 'I see,' or, 'And what about——?' for Mrs Richardson didn't stop talking until they had made their way up the broad curving staircase to the first floor. Only then was there a pause in the narrative, and shrewd hazel eyes surveyed Jenny.

'I do hope you'll like it here, Jenny. It isn't as formal as some hospitals, more of a convalescent home, really, and not everyone fits into such an *unstructured* setting.'

'I shall do my best to fit in,' Jenny promised solemnly, but with an imp of mischief dancing in her eyes, and the secretary chortled.

'Yes, I think you and Ben will get along very well. Dr Arifuddin said you're just what Ben needs,' Babs said enigmatically, then, after a brief introduction, she left Jenny to be greeted by the nursing manager, Fay Whalley.

Late April sunlight flooded the big, pleasantly furnished room as Mrs Whalley came forward to shake hands. 'Welcome to the Easterwood, Sister. We're one big happy family here, and I'm sure you will enjoy working with, and for, our patients.'

Jenny took the chair offered and watched through narrowed eyes as Fay Whalley seated herself behind an ancient mahogany desk. Despite her welcoming words, Mrs Whalley's smile was cool, a trifle wary, Jenny thought, compared with the good humour exuding from Babs Richardson. Then she dismissed the idea as fanciful. Why should the woman be wary of her?

'This office door is always open, to staff as well as patients, though you'll not see much of me on nights, of course,' Mrs Whalley was saying. 'I'm Fay, by the way. Ben—Dr Moran—likes a certain amount of informality, though all the patients call him Dr Ben.

Now. . .' She paused and glanced down at the desk, while a rather impatient Jenny waited and wondered. If there was something Fay wanted to say, why in heaven's name didn't she say it?

Then pale eyes caught Jenny in their beam and what seemed a reluctant smile touched Fay Whalley's thin lips. 'I'll take you to the sister's office. They should be finishing the hand-over now, and Marie—that's the day sister—can answer your questions about patients, treatments, and so on. I hope you will fit in here, Sister,' she added, echoing Babs Richardson's words earlier. 'You haven't had any experience of the *private* sector, I believe?'

'I thought the Easterwood was run by the NHS,' Jenny said, refusing to be ruffled, 'though I understand it's partly founded by private sources.' She had gleaned that much from Dr Arifuddin, Dr Moran's deputy.

The nursing manager nodded. 'That's right, though all patients are treated free. It's an experiment and we're all hoping that it will continue, but we have to show results, meet quotas. . .' Her voice trailed away, and Jenny began to wonder what she had got herself into. Dr Moran had been abroad when she came for her interview, and Dr Arifuddin had said nothing about showing results. It sounded as if the Easterwood was being run as a business.

Fay Whalley seemed disinclined to say more, and it was a thoughtful Jenny who followed her along a richly carpeted corridor to a set of double white doors. Then, as they were about to enter the acute suite, Fay whispered, 'You will try and get on with Dr Moran, won't you? Our last night sister didn't. Not at first, anyway. They clashed on everything, or so it seemed to me. Then——' She hesitated.

'Then?' Jenny prompted. 'If there was bad feeling between them because the sister had ideas for improving things here, perhaps I ought to know about it? If

Dr Moran is the type who won't listen to nursing staff then I——'

'Oh, good gracious, no! It was nothing like that. They simply had different ideas, that was all. I'm sorry I mentioned it,' Fay said firmly, then led the way into the ward area, leaving Jenny more perplexed than ever. What had she got herself into? And would she have to christen the clinic director 'Ben the Unbearable'?

To her dismay, the reception she had been afforded by Fay was echoed by the nurses she met in the large, airy ward office. Everyone smiled and told her they were pleased to see her, but it was one of the games people played, something familiar to any psychiatric nurse. She most definitely did *not* feel welcome, but she tried to put aside the faint feeling of unease. If there was some mystery to be unravelled, she would have plenty of time to do so on nights. It would be a challenge!

The day sister, Marie Thomson, seemed about the friendliest face, and she left the hand-over to escort Jenny round the clinic, or as much of it as was relevant for the time being.

Sister Thomson was in her mid-thirties, Jenny judged, a tall, capable-looking woman who looked as if nothing would ruffle her. 'I always think there's something special about nights,' she was saying as she led Jenny along another thickly carpeted corridor. 'I used to do them, but after a while I found I couldn't sleep during the day. Then my husband and I split up and nothing seemed to be going right.' She shrugged. 'Anyway, I've been firmly fixed on day duty for a couple of years now *and* I've got my private life better organised,' she confided, leading the way into a small, cosy sitting-room.

'This is one of several dayrooms. We keep them small because patients prefer it that way.' Marie lowered her voice, though the room was empty. 'Usually there are one or two patients about but most are at breakfast at the moment. You'll meet them later. Is this your first actual clinic?'

Jenny admitted that it was. 'If, by clinic, you mean a separate building set in gorgeous surroundings! I've been agency nursing recently,' she went on slowly, memory stirring, 'but my last sister's post was in one of those Victorian asylums the popular Press are always on about. I was happy there,' she added, surprising herself. Yes, for most of her stay, she had known a kind of happiness in doing a useful job that not many people would want to do. Known a certain tranquillity, too, despite the drab surroundings. But that was before. . . Her grey eyes darkened for a moment before she pushed the unacceptable memories away.

'I've worked in places like that, too,' Marie commented, apparently unaware of Jenny's anguish. 'But the Easterwood is something special. The house by itself is therapeutic. Do you know what I mean?'

'Yes, I felt it the moment I came for interview. It's funny,' Jenny went on slowly, 'but I felt as if I'd come home. It's an odd mixture of periods, though, isn't it? I convinced myself the house was Georgian but I'm not sure any more!'

'You aren't the only one who's perplexed! An old mansion once stood on the site, or so Ben told me, but this house dates from Edwardian times, I believe. Or Victorian. Ben would tell you; he's an expert. Naturally,' Marie added, but before Jenny could ask her what she meant Marie led the way into what must have been a formal reception-room in Edwardian days.

It was an almost square room, with another of the huge fireplaces Jenny had seen in the hall, and a carved mantelpiece. A many-leaved dining table held pride of place in the middle of the room, and seated around it were three women, somehow contriving to look perfectly at ease, despite the fact that large areas of table separated each one from her neighbour.

'I've brought the new night sister to meet you all,' Marie announced briskly. 'This is Sister Jenny Fraser, and these ladies are Helen, Mildred and Sophie.'

'Good morning, ladies. I hope I'm not disturbing your breakfast,' Jenny said smilingly. Although one woman ignored her completely, two pairs of eyes surveyed her carefully before the youngest of the trio spoke. She rose and came padding across the room in bare feet. Unlike the others, who were dressed, she wore a flowing silk caftan and a matching turban.

'Hello, Jenny. I'm Sophie Clary.' She held out both slim hands in welcome and Jenny took them. Sophie looked about eighteen or nineteen but could have been older. Her face was unlined, her expression dreamy, her eyes a beautiful turquoise blue, but they didn't quite meet Jenny's direct gaze. Rather, they looked through her. 'I'm sure you'll like it here. I do,' the girl went on ingenuously, and one of the others snorted.

'At least you've come willingly,' Mildred put in. She had newly permed grey hair, but looked old enough to be Sophie's grandmother, and lines of suffering were etched deep into her face. 'I can't wait to get back to civilisation,' she complained, and Sophie giggled.

'Pay no attention to her, Jenny! She's just upset because dear Dr Ben says she's got to go home. Do you play tennis?' Sophie went on, but Jenny shook her head.

'Not now. I played at school but I haven't bothered since.' Lloyd had played squash, something she had never cared for. Her own preference was for long walks with the family dog, the theatre, music. Rather dull for someone like Sophie.

'Perhaps we can find something we both enjoy,' Jenny suggested, but Sophie appeared to lose interest, and wandered back to her place. She stared down at her bowl of cereal for a long moment, watched carefully by Jenny, then padded out of the door at the opposite end of the room. Getting through that schizophrenic-like barrier was going to be another challenge. They were coming thick and fast!

The third patient, Helen, was lost in her own world, and Marie didn't linger. She said as she closed the door softly behind her, 'Helen Cross, manic-depressive psychosis. She's better than she was, though. I'll bring you up to date with them all when we've time. I'll just take you through here——' She opened a door a little way further along the corridor. 'Here we've got the nitty-gritty—interview-room, treatment-room, Night Sister's office. The staff canteen is separate, though. We eat in one of the cottages in the grounds. Rather nice. But that's only on days. There's a night dining-room on the ground floor, so you won't have to prowl around in the dark!'

'As you've done nights, is there any particular routine?' Jenny wanted to know, as they retraced their steps. 'Or do I just play it by ear? I did nights on an internal rotation at my last hospital, and I found the nights busier than the days!'

'Ye-es,' Marie said slowly. 'I think you'll find that here. One or two of them are great nocturnal wanderers. I think play it by ear is the best thing for a week or two. You'll be sharing the office with Sister Astley for the first night, and she'll ease you in gently. You've met her?' Marie wanted to know.

'Is that the German sister? Yes, I met her at the interview.' The sister had greeted Jenny with a beaming smile and a vigorous handshake. Certainly nothing unwelcoming about *her*.

'That's Resi—her husband's English, though. That's why she's settled here. She'll go out of her way to make you feel welcome,' Marie added. She paused as they stood in the archway which divided patient quarters from the doctors' rooms, and Jenny waited, wondering whether she was to hear the reason for the puzzling attitude of the other staff, but the moment passed, and Marie quickly completed the tour.

'Staff have their own toilets and washrooms. We keep them locked. In case of accidents,' Marie added, but it was unnecessary. 'Sophie Clary is suicidal, by the way. At least, she makes attempts. The last one was just before Christmas, and we nearly lost her then. But Ben, Dr Moran, doesn't think she means to do away with herself really.'

Jenny smiled grimly. 'Sometimes they *do* succeed by accident,' she put in. 'I take it Sophie's a regular? She seems to be at home here.'

'Yes, this is her second admission this year and we're not out of April yet! She hears voices. At least she *says* she does, but I'm not convinced she does actually hear them, poor dear. Anyway, I think that's all. I hope so,' Marie added with a little laugh. 'I'm getting quite dry! Oh, the bedrooms. I expect you saw them at interview?'

'Yes, I had a quick guided tour,' Jenny agreed. She had been glad to see that patients had bedrooms, rather than dormitories as in her previous hospital. She would have preferred to see more single accommodation, but that was a matter she could broach once she had settled in.

'Oh, about single rooms,' Marie cut into Jenny's thoughts. 'If any patient asks for a single room the moment he or she arrives, you'll have to be firm. We're informal here and try to make the place homelike, but single rooms aren't clinic policy, and all policies are for the patient's own good in the long run,' she finished, almost as though she had learned a script.

And perhaps she had, Jenny thought. A clear case of programming the staff! 'I should have thought——' she began, but her sentence was interrupted by a series of short but piercing screams. She tensed, ready to dash to the patient's aid, but Marie just listened, her head on one side.

'That's Sophie.' Without another word, the sister strode back towards the dining-room, Jenny hard on her heels. She only hoped Sophie Clary wasn't going to choose this morning to make a suicide attempt!

Another member of staff heard Sophie's distinctive screams, and he rose unhurriedly, surprised to hear her screaming but convinced that it was nothing serious.

He reached Sophie before Sister Thomson did, for the simple reason that she was sitting on the floor outside his office. 'You could always knock,' Ben Moran said quietly. 'Noisy women give me a headache.'

Sophie looked up, her eyes far-away, and Ben rather thought she couldn't see him. With Sophie, it was difficult to say. Just when he thought she had one particular psychiatric illness, she exhibited the symptoms of another one. It was bad practice to stick labels on psychiatric patients but it certainly helped.

Ben hunkered down beside her, knowing he looked big and intimidating when he stood up. 'Can you hear me, Sophie?'

The screaming died to a whimper, and soft tears rolled down the girl's cheeks. Her expression was still vague and far-away, as though she was listening to another voice inside her head.

Gently, Ben stroked her hair. It needed washing. Sophie mustn't be allowed to neglect herself. In some ways, she reminded him of Louise. Then, angry with himself for letting Louise into his thoughts, he got up. 'When you're feeling more yourself, come and talk to me. OK?'

It was at that moment that Marie sailed into view, a tall, fair-haired young woman with her, and Ben's eyes narrowed for a moment, Surely *she* wasn't the new night sister? But, yes, she sported a name badge on her stylish jacket.

A man who didn't much mind what he wore, Ben could yet appreciate style in others, and this lady had that in abundance. But she was younger than he'd expected. Pretty, too, in a fragile sort of way. Angelic, if you liked that type of woman, but he didn't.

What was Les Arifuddin doing, taking on someone like that? The job called for maturity, and he'd had in mind someone like Marie. After the last night sister, he certanly didn't want any romantically inclined blondes!

Jenny came to an abrupt halt, uncertainty shadowing her eyes as she met the assessing gaze of the man in the doorway. This surely wasn't Dr Moran? Ben the Unbearable? She had expected a much older man, and, from the expression on his handsome face, she wasn't what *he* had expected, either!

Marie made the introduction, and Jenny forced herself to offer her hand, together with the cool, capable smile expected of a ward sister. Dr Moran's handshake was firm yet gentle for so big a man. Then he smiled, his dark gaze holding hers, and a shaken Jenny was uneasily aware of his potent charm.

But the moment passed, and Marie helped Sophie Clary to her feet and ushered her away, leaving a faintly apprehensive Jenny to the mercy of the consultant psychiatrist.

'Won't you come in? Sit down, relax,' Dr Moran offered, suiting his actions to his words by sinking into a squashy-looking armchair, his pose as casual as the clothes he wore.

Jenny, who had never before seen a consultant in jeans and sweatshirt, looked about for a straight-backed chair, then realised it would be cowardly. If he could relax, so could she, so she took the other armchair, trying not to stare too obviously at the man opposite.

Lloyd was good-looking, but—— No, Lloyd was handsome. Conventionally so, but his almost perfect looks and bone-structure paled beside the magnificence of this man. There was something primeval about him. Frightening in a way, Jenny mused fancifully. No, not that. Dangerous. Sensuous. That's a silly word, she thought swiftly, hoping he wasn't summing *her* up, but knowing he would be. I must be going crazy. He's a consultant, for heaven's sake! A *psychiatrist*. Not some warrior from aeons ago, come to drag me by the hair back to his cave!

'You look surprised to see me, Sister Fraser. What did you expect, horns and a tail?' Dr Moran broke the silence, his slight accent puzzling Jenny for a moment.

She flushed, guiltily aware of her thoughts. 'I expected an older man,' she admitted, unable to tell him that someone had mentioned that Dr Moran walked with a slight limp at times and that it was an old war wound. That remark had conjured up visions of the Second World War, and she had expected a rotund, balding man with specs, almost ready for retirement. Whatever age Dr Moran was, he certainly wasn't rotund and balding! Oh, boy, was he not!

'I expected—and wanted—a rather older night sister,' Ben Moran said, his engaging smile robbing the words of offence. 'So we're both disappointed, but never mind.' He dismissed the problem lightly.

'I see,' said Jenny, rather miffed. Now she was too young! 'I *am* twenty-seven and perfectly capable, Doctor. If Dr Arifuddin didn't think I was too young for the post, perhaps he was right?' she suggested, tilting her little chin defiantly.

'Yes, maybe he was,' Ben admitted, liking the display of spirit. Sister Fraser might not be so angelic, at that! 'Anyway, a belated welcome to Easterwood! I hope you'll be happy here,' he went on, meaning it. 'I am.'

'Thank you. Fay Whalley said working here was like being part of one big, happy family,' Jenny said, a little smile playing about the corners of her well-shaped mouth. That Mrs Whalley's manner had fallen far short of that ideal was something Jenny intended keeping to herself. At least Dr Moran appeared to be sincere in his welcome, so that was a bonus point!

'Your name has a Scots ring to it—would I be right?' Ben went on, wondering what had caused the little imp of amusement to shine out of his new sister's lovely eyes.

Jenny nodded, her nerves well under control now. So—Dr Moran was charismatic and excellent at putting people at their ease. That was his job, wasn't it? It didn't mean he posed a threat to her new-found independence, the security that this job offered. Forget Lloyd, she told herself. This man is nothing like him. Well, thank heavens for that!

'My grandfather was a Scot, from the Paisley area. I think of England as home, though I was born in Scotland and I visit my grandmother from time to time. She was down here recently,' Jenny added. That was a visit all of them would remember for a long time.

'You have family here? Parents, boyfriend?' Ben suggested, his gaze thoughtful. She was pretty; she must have a lover around some place.

Jenny hesitated. Did she have a family now? Even the old dog had died. 'My mother lives in London,' she said calmly. 'I'm the only girl but I have two married brothers. They don't live locally.' There was the faintest of challenges in her eyes, but that didn't stop Ben.

'No boyfriend?' he persisted, aware that he was probably treading on dangerous ground, but not giving a damn.

'No, no boyfriend, Doctor,' Jenny said sweetly. How

dared he pry into her private life? Of course it mattered to him that she wasn't engaged and wouldn't be leaving before she had really settled into the job, but she couldn't help resenting the questions nevertheless. At her interview his deputy had been far more tactful. 'Will there be anything else?' she asked, still in that same level tone, and, unexpectedly, the doctor chuckled.

'No more personal questions, if that's what you mean. Is there anything you want to ask me about the Easterwood?'

Jenny thought for a moment. 'I don't believe so. Dr Arifuddin answered most of my questions at the interview. I gather you take people with psychotic as well as hysterical illnesses?'

'That's right. We draw the line at psychopaths, though. As you're aware, it isn't really an illness, it's a personality defect. Most other categories of patients come here, and we have a thriving day-patient centre for folk with anxiety and the compulsive disorders.'

Ben rose unhurriedly and went over to stand by the window, as he continued, 'We're partly funded by the private sector, as I imagine you know?'

Jenny glanced over at him as he leaned lazily against the wall. 'Yes, so I've been told.' Quotas and deadlines, she thought sourly.

'We're also part of the National Health Service, and patients don't pay for the privilege of being treated in what, *I* think, are wonderful surroundings. We work hard to keep it that way,' Ben added.

'A healing atmosphere,' Jenny suggested.

'Yes, that's right.' His gaze was thoughtful. 'On nights, too, it's just as important to keep that "family atmosphere" in mind, if you like to call it that. Wasn't it Flo Nightingale who said that a hospital should do the patient no harm? Some psychiatric hospitals do that, I'm afraid. The wonder of it is that people actually get better in such places. We have a high success rate at the Easterwood and I intend that it should stay that way.' He sounded oddly defiant—as if he expected Jenny to argue the point.

'I'll bear that in mind, Doctor,' she said, nettled by his apparent assumption that she needed reminding.

'Good.' The tenseness seemed to leave him, and that engaging grin broke out again. Jenny found herself responding by smiling back, forgetting for a moment that she must strive to keep a distance between herself and attractive men, even attractive *married* men, for surely Dr Moran must have a wife in the background? The legacy of bitterness left by Lloyd's behaviour was an enduring one.

She hesitated for a moment, aware that it was none of her business. 'I've been trying to place your accent, Dr Moran—it sounds faintly Australian, but——'

'Faintly Australian! Very faint, I should think,' Ben admitted. 'I haven't been back for quite some time.' His expression was grim. 'I think of England as home now, and I was actually born here. Now,' he said, with an abrupt change of subject, 'has Marie told you anything about our patients?'

'No, not yet. She was giving me a guided tour when we heard Sophie scream. I gather Sophie's suicidal, but what else?'

'I dislike sticking labels on people, Jenny. Let's just say Sophie's Sophie and leave it at that for the time being.' His tone was dismissive, and Jenny bridled. 'I'll give you a run-down on most of them some time but right now I have a meeting to attend. We hold a lot of meetings here, as you'll find.'

He watched as Jenny struggled up from the low armchair, wondering briefly if her lips were as kissable as they looked. 'Patients like talking about themselves, as you know, and we think it helps. They like to feel they've some say in their own treatment. Sometimes they can talk out a solution to their own problems, while we just offer support.'.

Jenny couldn't find fault with that, and she murmured her thanks as the psychiatrist held open the door for her.

She walked sedately back along the corridor, unaware that his eyes were following her. So that was the director of the Easterwood Clinic! A man to be wary of, she decided—*very* wary!

CHAPTER TWO

'WE HAVE twenty-four in-patients at present, plus the day people, of course,' Marie Thomson was saying, and Jenny brought her wandering thoughts back to the matter in hand. That brush earlier with Dr Moran had unnerved her, though why she had no idea. Perhaps it was something about those haunting dark eyes. She really must try to shake off this feeling about him.

'Quite a lot of them are acute anxiety and compulsive states, I gather,' she said crisply, and Marie nodded.

'Though they're a mixture, just like the rest of us. A patient might show signs of anxiety but she's probably depressed as well, or just unhappy. Only two are suicidal that we know of, and one of them's Sophie Clary. But that doesn't mean that some of the others won't make an attempt,' Marie went on.

'Mm, I know. I had a patient once who was an exhibitionistic type, always exaggerating, always telling us how sad she was that her husband had turned her out of the house, how she loved him and couldn't live without him—you know the sort of person,' Jenny said. 'Once or twice she mentioned ending it all, saying that she had nothing to live for, but none of us believed she would make a serious attempt. She loved herself too much. And it was, still is, difficult to believe she ever loved her husband. Anyway, she went over a cliff one morning. It was a highly successful attempt,' she finished drily.

'I suppose you still feel guilty about it?' Marie suggested, and Jenny gave a wry smile.

'You bet I do! We all did, for a time. We felt we had

24

failed her, and of course we *had*. We didn't listen properly. It certainly taught me a lesson!'

'I think we've all had experiences like that. Even psychiatrists aren't infallible, Jenny, so I don't see how nurses can expect to be. Forget it, chalk it up to experience and try to make sure you don't lose anybody else,' Marie advised.

That was easier said than done, but Marie knew that as well as she did. It was a fact of life for psychiatric nurses and it helped no one if the nurse took a failure like that too much to heart.

'How many men do you have? I've seen only one so far, a man in his seventies, I should think. A Mr Farrant,' Jenny said.

'Yes, that's Reggie. He lost his wife recently, and his daughter—and the GP thought a spell in the Easterwood would do him good, but it isn't the answer really. We can't bring back his wife, though we can give him support, help him to grieve properly.'

'That's the trouble outside. People are told to stop crying, put the past behind them. P——'

'Pull themselves together!' Marie and Jenny spoke as one, then exchanged knowing glances.

How often were sufferers told *that*? Jenny wondered.

Marie continued down the list of patients, only five of whom were men. Some were just in for a rest before returning to a way of life that was causing the symptoms of nervous illness. Many were depressed, mostly depression of the reactive variety, like Mr Farrant's, but there was Helen Cross with a more severe type of depression.

'We've got her over the period where she was full of concrete and said she was dead,' Marie told her, handing over Helen's case folder. 'She doesn't mention death now, and she can safely be left alone, at least in theory, but we don't take any chances, of course. We've always got a nurse to keep an eye on her, unless she's with others. Thank goodness, we've got a good nurse-patient ratio. She and Sophie get on well, surprisingly. I think it does Sophie good to have someone else to help, but. . .' Marie shrugged as if saying that Sophie was still a problem, and Jenny could well believe that.

'It says in her notes that she's got anorexia nervosa. Does she eat at all without coaxing?'

'Sophie? Well, she *does* eat. She's thin as a rake, as you've seen, but we——'

'Sorry to interrupt.' Dr Moran hovered in the doorway of the office, looking anything but sorry, and Jenny was amused to see Marie blossom under his disarming smile. Well, *she* wouldn't be doing any blossoming! 'I'm just going to interview the new patient and I thought Sister Fraser might like to sit in on the interview,' Ben Moran went on.

Jenny rose, glad of the chance to do something constructive. Learning about the various patients was all-important, but she had names and illnesses coming out of her ears. It was too much to absorb in one day, and she welcomed the chance to be in at the beginning with a patient.

Dr Moran's long strides had already taken him halfway along the corridor as Jenny emerged from the office, and she saw that there was little trace of a limp. He might at least have waited for her, though. She quickened her pace, sliding easily into the brisk nurse's walk that she had spent nine years perfecting.

He glanced back, his eyes hooded. 'There's no need to run, Jenny. We have all day.'

Exasperated, Jenny bit back the tart retort and smiled instead. The smile lit up her thin face, and Ben thought the sun had come out again. Whoever that guy was who'd given her the run-around, he was all kinds of a fool!

'I didn't expect you to wait for me,' she said glibly. 'I have long legs and I'm used to striding out.'

'Yes, they are long. You've got a neat pair of ankles, too,' Ben observed, and she gasped.

He paused, leaning against the dividing archway. His smile was lop-sided. Engaging, really, if you liked that sort of thing, but Jenny assured herself she didn't. 'Not going to accuse me of sexism, are you?' Ben asked, dark eyes mocking her.

'No, of course not, Doctor! That sort of thing's overdone, and thank you for the compliment,' Jenny managed, longing to say something outrageous to wipe that cheeky grin from his face.

Ben inclined his head. 'It was a pleasure. At least I won't have to call you Fraser the Feminist, will I? By the way,' he went on before Jenny could respond, 'call me Ben—Ben the Buccaneer,' he added, and Jenny smiled. She'd heard the nickname from Marie, though she thought the sister had been unaware of using it. Well, it suited him!

'Tell me about the new patient, Dr—Ben. I know I mustn't stick labels on them but it does help to know what he or she is suffering from,' she went on quickly.

'*Touché*.' Ben's expression was wry. 'Come on in and I'll tell you all about her.'

Somewhat alarmed, Jenny entered his psychiatrist's office for the second time that day. This time, though, she kept well away from the comfortable armchairs, and chose a ladder-backed chair over by the window.

Ben's windows overlooked the formal gardens at the rear of the house, and Jenny's gaze was drawn to the sunshine outside, and to the patients strolling, some arm in arm, or just sitting on the benches or on the terrace below.

One or two were standing completely still, lost in introspection and oblivious to the warm spring day. Steps led down from the terrace on the floor below, and a wide expanse of lawn stretched as far as Jenny could see. To the left there was a knot garden, and, further still, she saw the glint of sunlight on water.

'You have a lovely situation here,' she commented, turning reluctantly from the view. 'It's far better than my last hospital—one of those grim Victorian buildings.'

'Yes, I've worked in one or two,' Ben admitted, his gaze assessing. 'There's nowhere like the Easterwood.' He paused, and Jenny wondered what was coming next. 'What made you leave your last hospital? You told Les it was to further your career, but is that all it was? I'd hazard a guess that there's a man responsible for the move somewhere along the line.' His tone was cold.

Flustered by his perceptiveness, Jenny was at a loss for words for a moment. 'I can assure you that I *do* want to further my career! I have plans for my future and——'

She was saved by the bell. With a grunt of annoyance, Ben reached out to answer the telephone, then his expression changed.

Jenny watched, amazed, as he positively oozed charm down the phone. A private patient, perhaps, she thought unfairly, though such a straight-talking man didn't seem the type to tug his forelock to private patients—not to anybody, come to that!

'Yes, I'll be home by six. No, I can't make it before then, you know that. Yes, I'll try.' Ben was still smiling as he replaced the receiver, but his shrewd gaze was resting on Jenny, who moved uneasily, aware that her expression might have given away more than she had intended.

'A friend,' he said easily, then picked up the case-notes on the new patient, apparently dismissing the caller from his mind.

A friend, indeed! Jenny almost snorted. But if he

had a live-in lover, that was his business. Just as Lloyd
Simmons and her reasons for leaving London were
hers. At least Ben had dropped *that* line of enquiry
now.

'Mrs Stella Lawrence,' Ben read out, startling her
out of her reverie. 'Aged forty-nine, just starting the
menopause. She's developing an obsessive-compulsive
illness.' He paused and looked at Jenny, one heavy
eyebrow raised. 'Are you still with me, Jenny?'

'Of course,' she answered calmly. He saw too much,
that was his trouble! But, of course, psychiatrists did;
it was part of their job. 'Has it come out of the blue?'
she wondered aloud. 'And has the menopause any
bearing on it?'

'That's something we'll have to find out. But as to it
coming out of the blue, her GP says what we would
suspect—that she's always been obsessively tidy, not
liking anything out of place, always plumping up cushions and setting them exactly in line—you know the
type?' Ben smiled easily at her and Jenny tried not to
notice how the smile lit up his rather stern features,
making the Buccaneer look years younger than he
probably was. Those deep-set eyes, too, were smiling,
and Jenny swiftly looked away, apparently deep in
thought.

'I've nursed quite a few patients of that type, certainly,' she agreed at last. 'They were usually day
patients, though. At my last hospital they thought
treating them on an in-patient basis would be self-
defeating. You don't feel that?'

Ben considered. 'I think it depends very largely upon
the patient and upon the facilities available. This lady
is all geared up to come and stay a while. If we tell her
she has to come daily or weekly, she probably won't
make the effort, and we're off the beaten track,
anyway. There's a lot to be said for treating obsessive
patients in the community, but this whole house is

therapeutic. A rest away from the pressures of life might be just what Mrs Lawrence needs. Who knows?' He got up suddenly, his lazy smile warming her. 'Shall we see the lady?'

Stella Lawrence proved to be a thin lady with greying hair, carefully rinsed. She was tall, taller even than Jenny, and quite attractive, though the harassed expression on her face detracted from this. When she smiled, only her mouth made the effort. Her eyes, a light, watery blue, remained cold and wary. Not an easy person to get to know, Jenny mused, as the three of them made themselves comfortable in the interview-room.

This room overlooked the front of the clinic but, like the rest of the acute suite, was on the first floor and away from distractions. It was pleasantly furnished with curtains of a bright, cheerful pattern and one or two small prints on the walls. A vase full of tulips stood on the side-table, there were magazines in a rack by the door, and plenty of armchairs complete with cushions, to give the room the air of a family living-room, as, presumably, it had once been.

The air of slightly untidy normality about the room seemed to agitate Mrs Lawrence, who adjusted the cushion before perching on the edge of a chair, then got up again to re-adjust the cushion. It was only to be expected that she would be ill at ease. A first interview was never easy, except when the patient was so profoundly depressed that nothing made any impact, but Jenny felt it was more than that. Mrs Lawrence might have been fighting down the urge to tidy the room, taking the curtains and covers away to wash. It was behaviour that they would have expected from her.

'Your doctor tells me you would like to come in for a few days,' Ben began, getting to the point as usual, and the woman shrugged.

'Well—he thinks it might be a good idea, but I'm

not so sure. . .' She shot a quick glance at Jenny. 'I
don't want to be rude, but does Sister have to stay? I
hoped we could have a chat, just the two of us, you
know,' she hurried on, and Jenny smiled easily.

'I know what you mean, Mrs Lawrence,' she agreed.
'It's often easier to relate just to one person at a time.'

'Yes, that's right.' Mrs Lawrence's eyes were fixed
appealingly on the psychiatrist.

'It's usual to have a nurse present,' Ben said blandly.
He could have seen her alone, of course. In her own
home, he would probably have done so, but he preferred not to. Experience had taught him to be wary of
his own attractiveness to women. He couldn't afford to
be alone with a female patient of the kind he judged
Mrs Lawrence to be.

'If you would like it better, I could make arrangements for Dr Forster to be here next time,' he suggested. 'But Sister Fraser's going to be in charge on
nights for part of the week, and she needs to get to
know our patients. Being in at the beginning is helpful
for her as well as for you,' he pointed out, his charming
smile clearly weakening the woman's resolve to be seen
alone. 'But. . .' He paused dramatically, and Mrs
Lawrence made a moue.

'If it's usual, then of course Sister must stay, but Dr
Forster used to see my niece without a chaperon.'

Neither Ben nor Jenny commented, Ben reflecting
that Dr Forster, one of the part-time psychiatrists at
the Easterwood, was nearing retirement and had no
need to be chaperoned, Jenny thinking that Ben Moran
was a victim of his own charm—he *needed* protection!

Ben didn't pick up the point about the niece being
seen by a psychiatrist and Jenny wondered why. Surely
that was of importance? Any familial tendency towards
mental illness or just plain obsessiveness ought to be
investigated. Instead, he appeared to lose control of

the interview, letting the conversation veer wherever it would, though Jenny realised that this was deliberate.

Once or twice he put a question to Mrs Lawrence, but most of the time it wasn't necessary. She clearly loved talking, though not about herself, and Ben let her talk, picking up clues from what she didn't say as much as from what she did. Body language, too, helped in a diagnosis, and Jenny watched with an expert eye as Mrs Lawrence waved her hands expressively, and shuffled her feet from time to time, but mostly she kept her legs close together, her slender ankles crossed. Once she tried to pull down her skirt, though it was longer than Jenny wore hers and certainly covered her knees. Then she fiddled with her wedding and engagement rings, the latter a huge emerald that must have cost a fortune and was far too large for her small hands.

Although Mrs Lawrence was beautifully made-up, her hands were in complete contrast, being red and careworn due to the frequent washing and even scrubbing they suffered.

'Do you think you would be happy without your symptoms?' Ben threw in carelessly as the interview was drawing to its conclusion, and the woman opened her eyes wide in apparent astonishment.

'Of *course*! I—I feel happy once I've completed the rituals, but——' She hesitated, and they waited. 'Then I become unhappy again until I've gone through it all again. The washing, the straightening out of creases. Then I have to bath and wash my hands, keep washing my hands. . .' Her voice trailed away as she, too, glanced down at the tell-tale hands, before hiding them behind her handbag. Then quickly she changed the subject, mentioning her husband for the first time. 'Something in the City, always wheeling and dealing,' was how he was dismissed, Mrs Lawrence hurrying on to talk about a holiday she'd had recently in the Greek islands.

'You look Greek, Doctor. Are you?' she asked bluntly, and Ben smiled easily.

'I'm Australian, but yes, you're partly right. My mother was English, but my grandmother was Greek,' he admitted.

That explained the dramatic darkness of the man, Jenny reflected as she saw Mrs Lawrence out of the room and into the care of the nurse who would make arrangements for her admission shortly. That hardly explained the war wound, though, unless Ben had been practising in some war-torn part of the world. It could be the case—he looked tough enough to cope with that kind of life. Ben the Greek Buccaneer. She tensed as the Buccaneer himself caught up with her, as she made her way towards the small house where the second lunch would be ready.

'Nearly time to put on the feeding-bag, I think,' he remarked, and Jenny nodded.

'I could eat a horse, feeding-bag and all!' she announced, and Ben chuckled. It was a husky chuckle and she liked the sound. Anxious to get back on a business footing, she said, 'I hope I proved to be an adequate chaperon?'

'You managed beautifully, Jenny. Thanks. Sometimes I wish I was short and fat with steel-rimmed spectacles!'

That was too much. 'I'm sure you wish nothing of the sort!' she retorted. 'Handsome men enjoy being handsome, like being sought after,' she added with a rare tactlessness.

'He was handsome, was he? That guy who threw you over?' Ben suggested, a smug note in his voice to which Jenny objected.

She refused to answer, and totally ignored him when he chuckled. The man was unsufferable! Quite insufferable—and quite right, she added silently. Lloyd *was* handsome *and* enjoyed the adulation that his good looks brought.

'Have you worked here long?' she asked instead, her mind going off on a different tack, and he seemed surprised by the question.

'A little over four years. I worked at the Maudsley for a while before that, but in between I went overseas.' He shrugged. 'Nothing worked out the way I planned it.'

There was a wary note in his voice now, and Jenny wondered at it. Perhaps, like her, the doctor had something to hide, a skeleton in his closet which he didn't like to hear rattled.

They were at the cottage now, and Jenny thought it had probably once been a staff cottage, perhaps for a married butler or steward. Another cottage housed the main admin offices, except for the nursing manager's suite. 'The 'Big House', as it was irreverently called, was kept for patients, treatments and reception.

Ben stood aside to let Jenny enter first. 'The food's good,' he commented. 'All home-grown and home-cooked, none of this "chips with everything" kind of menu! We get waited on, too,' he added with that warm smile that Jenny was beginning to find so disturbing.

She didn't respond to the smile, merely walked ahead of him, seeking out a table which she could share with other nursing staff. She certainly didn't expect him to follow her and take the seat next to her at a table which was just big enough for four. His long legs stretched out opposite hers, and Jenny had to move her own to make way for them, being careful that her feet didn't touch his.

Feeling acutely uncomfortable, she searched her mind for something innocuous to say, but, finding nothing, remained silent. Instead, she gazed about her with interest. The cottage was bigger than it looked from the outside, and the dining-room held perhaps seven or eight tables, each spread with a fresh white tablecloth and sparkling cutlery. Most tables were for four but Jenny saw several in an adjoining room which were set for two people only, and Ben's eyes followed hers.

'That's where the fine folks sit—GPs, visiting specialists and so on,' he explained, and Jenny's mouth quivered as she tried not to smile. She was determined not to be drawn into the trap of feeling relaxed in Ben's presence. His charm was of the dangerous variety.

'And you're not one of the fine folks?' she countered.

Ben shook his head, then smoothed back a wayward lock of hair. 'I sit with the masses,' he said, tongue-in-cheek, and Jenny couldn't keep back the laughter which bubbled up inside her.

'That's better. Much better,' Ben applauded. 'A laugh a day keeps the shrink away. Isn't that the saying? You look as if you used to laugh a lot,' he went on thoughtfully, and Jenny flushed, well aware that her heightened colour was obvious because of her fair skin.

'I laugh when there's something to laugh at,' she said quietly, refusing to be drawn into an indiscreet remark. Then the starter arrived, a deliciously aromatic home-made soup for herself, and orange juice for Ben.

'If it helps to talk about it, I'm always here, Jenny,' he said softly, and she glanced up, ready to assure him that she solved her own problems.

Something in his eyes stopped her, though, and she merely nodded, at the same time wishing she *could* confide in him.

Then a pleasantly low-pitched voice asked if she might join them, and Jenny glanced up—to meet the cool gaze of a tiny, slender woman in an elegant grey suit.

Ben made the introductions, a slight smile on his wide mouth. 'This is our new night sister, Jenny Fraser. She's partly Scots, like haggis,' he drawled. 'Jenny, I'd like you to meet Rachel Bonner. Rachel's our senior behavioural nurse therapist.'

Jenny and Rachel exchanged smiles. On Jenny's part, it was a warm smile. After all, she might have to work with the woman and, even if the other staff were wary of *her*, she had no reason to be wary of any of them.

Rachel had hair so dramatically black that it couldn't have been its natural colour. It was plaited and held in place on the top of her head by a comb studded with brilliants. She wasn't beautiful, far from it. She had rather a homely face, with laughter-lines at the corners of her eyes. A pleasant face, Jenny decided, hoping she might have found a friend. But Rachel's expression remained cool, her tawny green eyes watchful. Cat's eyes, Jenny thought in dismay, and this particular cat doesn't like me at all.

CHAPTER THREE

On Thursday evening, Jenny attended her first patients' meeting. Most of the patients were there, and she couldn't help contrasting it with the meetings they had held in her last hospital. There, it had taken much determination to get even a small group together. Often the excuse was offered that they were 'Waiting for the doctor, dear', or 'I've got visitors coming'. Or, even more ingenuous, 'Doctor said I needn't go to any more meetings'!

Jenny took her seat as part of a big semicircle. Whatever the doctors at the Easterwood thought about meetings, they certainly attended them. She counted three besides Ben, who would be coming along later.

Dr Arifuddin, his deputy, was in his forties, Jenny judged, a tall, spare man with a lively sense of humour and a kind smile. His brood of children were often to be seen about the clinic, since he and his wife lived in one of the cottages in the grounds. Dr Walter was young, a pleasantly fresh-faced man with a mop of curly hair and a great deal of charm. By contrast, Dr Forster was balding and about ready for retirement. He was a quiet, courteous man and Jenny took to him straight away.

She and David Forster were together now, with a patient either side of them. In Jenny's case, this was Peggy Jefferson, a rather manic lady, who, earlier in the day, had attempted to polish one of the priceless tables with black boot polish! She was also convinced she could fly, so needed careful watching by her own nurse. That task had fallen to Jenny for the late shift, and it wasn't proving easy.

Peggy leaned forward expectantly, her eyes over-bright, and Jenny tensed, ready for anything. Opposite sat Sophie Clary and a patient who had been re-admitted that morning, Anne Bomford. Evidently the two of them were old friends, and it boded ill for night duty. Unlike the majority of the patients, who would remain well once they were discharged, Sophie and Anne and a couple of others were a 'hard core' of people admitted again and again—something familiar to psychiatric nurses. Such patients required careful supervision, and Jenny had been perturbed to note that there wasn't much of that. The staff weren't slack, exactly, but. . .

She shrugged aside the feeling, determined that at night she would know *exactly* where everyone was.

Dr Arifuddin called the meeting to order, and quickly a patient was chosen to act as chairperson—Simon Jenkins, who had been admitted two days before. He was a sufferer from compulsions, and Jenny had spent part of the afternoon helping him fill in a questionnaire for Rachel Bonner. Unfortunately, they had both fallen foul of Rachel, and the other woman's attitude irked Jenny.

Simon proved excellent at leading the meeting, and Jenny carefully noted his patience and forbearance when Sophie began to giggle uncontrollably. And when Peggy got up to dance inside the circle, it was Simon who led her back to her seat. Jenny had been inclined to let the woman dance, since it would rid her of some of that surplus energy, but of course it was disturbing to the others.

'We're not here to watch that woman make an exhibition of herself!' another patient snapped, and Jenny caught hold of Peggy's hand.

'Sit still for a while, dear. We'll have a dance later,' she promised. 'I could do with some exercise.'

'Lovely,' murmured Peggy. 'Lovely.' She sat back

for a few minutes, then Ben appeared, and she began
to clap. This was taken up by everyone present, and a
surprised Ben bowed low to the meeting, amid ripples
of laughter.

Their RGN student was sitting a few seats away, and
Jenny watched with narrowed eyes as the girl turned a
fiery red because Ben chose to sit next to her. Another
conquest for the Buccaneer!

Ben didn't interfere with Simon's chairmanship, even
though everyone waited politely for any comment the
consultant might wish to make. He was in his usual
uniform of jeans, this time coupled with a blue and
white striped shirt and an elderly pullover that Jenny
thought belonged in the rag-bag. He leaned back
nonchalantly, relaxed, completely at his ease, and she
envied him.

She felt at home now he was there. Complete,
fulfilled. No! His presence made no difference whatso-
ever, she told herself. But it did to her manic patient,
who tried to get up again. Despite Jenny's gentle
firmness, Peggy was determined that she was going to
dance across to Ben, and that was what she did.

Ben took her hand, asked the still flushed student to
move up, and seated Peggy next to him. 'Do you want
to say anything to the meeting?' he asked gently, but
she shook her head, and Ben nodded to the chairman
to continue.

Apart from Sophie still laughing at intervals, the
meeting was taken over by the more sensible members
of the group, and Jenny found that plans were afoot
for an amateur talent contest, largely instigated by the
serious-minded Dr Forster.

Apart from the contest, there would be a play of
sorts, and musical entertainment, and everyone was
given a job to do, even Peggy and Sophie. Getting
even half the patients to do their allotted tasks would
take all the persistence and ingenuity of which the staff

were capable, and Jenny knew how mentally as well as physically tiring it would be.

But it was a lovely idea, and Jenny's head was full of plans as she left the meeting-room which was the former ballroom, crossed a seldom used room full of dust-sheeted furniture, then entered the main corridor.

Peggy waltzed along by her side, singing. She seemed happy enough but the happy state could suddenly turn manic and Jenny wasn't taking any chances.

'We'll dance in a minute, then you can have a nice cup of Ovaltine with me. After that, I must pack up—tomorrow's another day.'

'Silly Sister! Tomorrow is always another day,' Peggy murmured. 'I shall dance for them, shan't I? And Dr Forster whistles, you know,' she said chattily, as she followed Jenny into the office, kicked off her shoes and made herself comfortable, her long black skirt sweeping the floor.

'Does he?' a startled Jenny asked. 'I didn't know he was musical! Does Dr Ben do anything?' she went on, very anxious to know.

'I can recite Wordsworth's "Daffodils". Will that do?' a husky voice asked, and Peggy let out a trill of laughter, then patted her false hairpiece.

'Dear Dr Ben! I think Sister likes you. She was staring at you in the meeting,' Peggy went on, leaving a flustered Jenny to wish herself miles away.

'Really?' Ben murmured. 'Now that *is* interesting!' So, the cool, ladylike Sister Fraser liked looking at him. His smile was wry, and he didn't torment his new sister by looking directly at her. Next week was Louise's birthday. He mustn't forget that.

Remember Louise, he reflected. Just as Jenny thought, Beware of this man's charm. Remember Lloyd.

* * *

By the end of her orientation week, Jenny was beginning to find her way around the huge house and, more importantly, had developed a good working relationship with most, if not all, of the staff.

Whatever it was that had caused the day staff to be wary of her hadn't actually disappeared, but it was less obvious now, and Jenny wisely made no reference to it. Maybe they thought she would be a 'new broom sweeps clean' type of person, as perhaps her predecessor had been. Indeed, sometimes she had the urge to suggest different and, she felt, better ways of doing things, but she resisted the urge. Time enough to make her ideas felt when she was on nights. What the day staff did wasn't really her concern unless the patients suffered.

With most of the patients, too, she was soon at ease. Sophie Clary remained wary of her and unapproachable, but the girl was an enigma to most of the staff, anyway, only Ben Moran apparently understanding what made her tick.

Darn Ben Moran, she thought as she sat by the bed of a patient who had just undergone ECT. This was Friday morning, and the electro-convulsive therapy session or ECT had just finished, and Jenny had offered to sit with the day patients, many of whom came in just for that treatment plus counselling sessions before and after.

Bridget Murray was on her last treatment, and she gazed up blankly at Jenny before her eyes focused properly. 'Oh, it's you, Sister! I couldn't think who you were for a moment,' she said drowsily as Jenny helped her to sit up.

Since these patients had undergone a general anaesthetic, they were treated as post-op patients in that respect, and Bridget had been placed in the recovery position after the treatment, with an airway in place, just as she would have been in the recovery-room of a general hospital.

'How do you feel?' Jenny asked gently, smoothing back the woman's grey-streaked hair. Bridget had periods of deep depression which came on without apparent cause, and this was her second course of ECT.

The patient considered for a moment. 'I'm not sure. I never feel really "here" after the shock treatment, but I'll be fine in a wee while. I know there's a nice cup of tea waiting, anyway! One I haven't had to make myself,' she added, and Jenny raised a brow. Because these people were day patients, they didn't come within her orbit, and their records were kept separately, so she knew nothing about the woman other than what she had been told by the staff nurse in charge—that Bridget would probably be back again before the year was out, perhaps as an in-patient.

'Do you live alone, Mrs Murray?' Jenny asked carefully, assisting the patient to sit in the wheelchair provided. 'I'll just whisk you away to the dayroom and your nice cuppa.'

'No, there's my family. I've two granddaughters, but they don't care about an old woman,' Bridget mumbled, but refused to be drawn further when Jenny suggested that one of the grandchildren be asked to make her a cup of tea sometimes.

Well, it was none of her business, and she knew only too well that it was unprofessional to become too involved with patients, but Jenny felt sorry for the woman, even though a depressed mother and grand-mother must be a burden for her family to bear, particularly as it was a recurring illness.

Once Bridget was settled happily next to someone she knew, Jenny was free for the rest of the morning. This afternoon there would be another of the many meetings Ben had warned her about on her first day, but for now she could read case-notes or sit and talk to the patients, and she was about to seek out Sophie, when she saw Ben Moran making his way determinedly in her direction.

'You look less than pleased to see me, Jenny,' he said laconically.

'I wish you wouldn't keep reading my mind,' she said crossly, and he smiled. It was a slow, sensuous smile, calculated to turn a girl's head or make her heart race just that little bit faster, but of course it didn't have that effect on her. Thanks to Lloyd, she was immune to sensuous looks from attractive men. 'As a matter of fact, I was hoping you hadn't found me something to do. I was going to look for Sophie Clary,' Jenny admitted. 'I thought the more rapport I can have with her now, the easier it will be on nights.'

'Nothing if not practical,' Ben commented. 'You don't look practical, Jennifer Fraser. You look. . .' He paused, while Jenny stood in the middle of the day-room, face flushed, eyes mutinous. 'You look ethereal, fragile, as though a puff of wind would knock you flying. But you're not. You're probably as tough as a pair of army boots,' he teased, and Jenny mockingly dropped a curtsy.

'Why, thank you, Doctor!' she purred. 'That's the nicest thing you've said to me all week!'

Ben threw back his head and laughed, and Jenny found herself joining in. Being likened to a pair of army boots wasn't exactly flattering, but he was right about her being tough. With two elder brothers determined to prove that 'Male was Mighty', she'd had to learn toughness from an early age!

It was unfortunate that Rachel Bonner chose that moment to sway into the dayroom, and she *did* sway. In a model, it would have been called a sensuous walk, and Jenny rather envied the woman. It was far more feminine than her own brisk stride.

'There you are, Ben, dear,' Rachel said, ignoring Jenny. 'I've just been talking to Simon Jenkins and I'd like your opinion. He hasn't finished all his tests yet, not by a long way,' she added meaningly, and Jenny tensed.

'I expect that remark was meant for me,' she said lightly, aware that she had inadvertently stepped on Rachel's dainty little toes. 'I'm sorry about the library, but I knew Simon wanted to keep busy. See you!' Jenny forced a smile to her face, and quickly headed towards the night sister's office, deciding that she would check the treatment charts before going in search of Sophie. Ben and Rachel were welcome to each other!

Poor Simon was forced to check whatever he had done umpteen times a day. Once he had finally left for work in the mornings, he had to go back again just to re-check everything. He was separated from his wife now, didn't see his nine-year-old daughter at all, and his job was in jeopardy—or would be, if he continued as he was.

Now, robbed of his routine and on extended sick leave, Simon was like a lost soul, and Jenny had quickly found him a job in the patients' library on the ground floor. It wasn't a made-up job. It was one that needed doing, and the librarian had been glad of his help.

Unfortunately, this had caused a low-key row with the forceful Rachel Bonner, who had wanted him to try out various forms of occupational therapy, until she had the time to give him her undivided attention.

Jenny's face clouded, then she shrugged aside the momentary irritation. She had the man's best interests at heart, but, she acknowledged, she was partly in the wrong and she ought to have asked Rachel's permission. Yet Simon had no time for his elaborate rituals while he was under the librarian's eye, so it might work out in the end. Still, she mustn't antagonise Rachel.

That was hardly an auspicious beginning to her career at the Easterwood!

Never mind; from next Monday she would be on nights and away from Rachel *and* Ben. Consultants kept fairly regular hours, except when they were making domiciliary visits, and she wouldn't be seeing Ben the Buccaneer for quite some time. Well, she was glad about *that*.

Her flat seemed an oasis of sweet silence after the noise of the clinic, and Jenny flopped down into her one easy chair the moment she got home. She had been lucky enough to find a furnished flat, which was not too far from the clinic yet far enough for her to feel that she wasn't 'living over the shop'. Here, in this Edwardian house, she could be free of the pressures that her work inevitably brought.

It had certainly been an eventful week, she mused as she stared straight ahead of her at the modern water-colour which her favourite sister-in-law had given her as a 'settling in' present. The picture depicted nothing in particular as far as she could see, but the colours were restful, a soothing blend of leaf-green, powder-blue and tendrils of silver. Modern art seemed to be a favourite with someone at the clinic, too, for in every room there was a water-colour, some of them painted by former patients, though these tended to be in darker, sombre colours. Of the oil-paintings which must once have hung over the mantelpieces in the reception-rooms there was now no sign. The house boasted a portrait gallery, but here, too, the paintings were modern, interspersed with weird-looking pieces of sculpture.

Wearily, Jenny closed her eyes, her temples throbbing with the beginnings of a headache. From now until Monday night she was a free agent, and there was absolutely nothing she wanted to do. Even her friends

were too far away for a visit, though she could always
phone one of them, of course.

Yet that idea didn't appeal at that particular
moment, and she made herself get up and strip off her
uniform. It had arrived in the middle of the week and
she was pleased with it. The crisp white zip-front dress
was cut on princess lines and flattered her rather too
thin figure. At the Easterwood, nurses still wore caps
and hers was of lace, as befitted a sister. Well, she
could dispense with *that* for a few hours, anyway!

Some of the staff, notably Rachel, wore their own
clothes, but Jenny had found that many patients preferred to see their nurses in uniform, and felt that the
sight of a uniform was reassuring, comforting. That
might not be such a good thing, though, she reflected,
then the shrilling of the doorbell broke into her
thoughts.

Her first thought was of Lloyd. Why that should be,
she didn't know. It was hardly likely he would turn up,
even if he knew where she was. But he *does* know.
Mum will have told him, a little voice whispered, and
Jenny said aloud, 'You're talking rubbish,' before
slipping into a housecoat then easing the door back on
its chain. It might be someone from the clinic, but——

It *was* someone from the clinic. The smiling
Buccaneer stood on her doorstep, and Jenny was sorely
tempted to close the door on him.

'Oh, hello! Is something the matter?' she said
instead, and Ben raised a brow, his eyes glinting.

'Should there be? Why are you wearing your dressing-gown? I've heard of early nights but this is
ridiculous!'

Belatedly aware that the housecoat was revealing
more of her undie-clad figure than she had intended,
Jenny flushed, the warm tide of colour suffusing her
cheeks, causing Ben to peer intently through the inch
gap of the door.

'I was wrong—army boots don't blush like that!'

'I am not blushing!' Jenny's voice was sharp. Here she was in her scanties, not even washed, her hair a mess, and yes, she *was* blushing! She felt like crying. Having older brothers had taught her never to do that, but the temptation was great.

'I'm taking you out to dinner. How about seven-thirty? That should give you time to get dressed,' Ben added meaningfully, still smiling at her.

To Jenny's surprise, he had changed those awful casual clothes for something rather more formal—a dark suit and white shirt and a tie. That wayward curl had remained untamed, though, and it gave him a boyish look quite at variance with the expression in his eyes.

She almost found herself agreeing that, yes, she could be ready by seven-thirty, but stopped just in time. 'Thank you for the invitation, Dr Moran, but I——'

'Ben,' he supplied helpfully, then sighed.

Jenny tried not to laugh. 'Ben, then. Thank you for the invitation, but I don't feel like going out to dinner. I'm exhausted, quite frankly,' she admitted. Well, that was no lie. A week in a new hospital was a very long time!

He shook his head, clearly not believing her. 'You're supposed to say you have to stay in and wash your hair,' he pointed out.

'Yes,' she agreed evenly, 'I could say that, but it wouldn't be true. I washed it this morning before I went on duty.'

'Ah, *that's* no good as an excuse, then.' Ben appeared to consider, while Jenny stood there, her face against the opening of the door. She was beginning to feel mean and spiteful and terribly guilty, and she resented it. She hadn't asked him to call, for heaven's sake! She could hardly close the door in his face, but, since she was determined not to go out, there was little point in continuing the somewhat one-sided conversation.

'I know!' Ben snapped his fingers, an unholy gleam in his eyes. 'You could come out for an hour or so, then tell me you have to phone your boyfriend! *That* will stop me from getting any fancy ideas,' he added, and she bit her lip, her temper getting the better of her.

'It's very kind of you to invite me out, Dr Moran, but *no*, I do *not* wish to come! I honestly don't feel like dining out,' she added, since his eyes now held a wistful expression, and she didn't want that expression coming back to haunt her during her solitary evening. It was unfair! Just because he was at a loose end, he was trying to take advantage of her good nature. Presumably his so-called 'friend' wasn't available this evening, so. . .

'Can't you find anyone else to dine with——?'

'I've got a better idea!'

They both spoke together, and Ben indicated that she could finish her sentence. She did so. 'Can't you find anyone else to dine with you? Someone from the clinic perhaps?' she hurried on, thinking of Rachel Bonner. Now there was a willing woman if ever she'd seen one!

He shrugged. 'Rachel's gone away for the weekend, but there's Marie—— No.' He shook his head regretfully. 'She's busy, she told me so herself. What about that new staff nurse? Now *she* isn't likely to be washing her hair tonight. Or there's——' He moved a little way away, grinning wolfishly.

'All right, all right! You win! I'll put on my glad rags and come out, but only for a couple of hours,' Jenny said, his persistence wearing her down. And she had to admit, but only to herself, that an evening in his company would be a darn sight more interesting than one spent gazing at the walls and thinking of Lloyd Simmons—dreaming of what might have been if it hadn't been for her mother's intervention.

'I've gone off the idea now—why don't you invite me in? There must be something in your store cupboard that you could make up, surely? A little home cooking is just what I need,' Ben assured her.

He stood there, a disturbing expression in his eyes, a little smile hovering about his somewhat ruthless mouth. She hadn't noticed it before. Oh, she'd decided that very first day that it was a well-shaped mouth, and that he had lovely teeth. Big teeth, she thought. But the hint of ruthlessness had escaped her until now. Not a man to cross.

But she was able to play her trump card. 'I don't like cooking, and I'm not very good at it. The most I could offer you is spaghetti bolognese with some sort of starter.'

The smile deepened. 'Sounds great! Do I get to come in, or will you feed me through the gap?'

Jenny's sense of humour came to her rescue, and laughter bubbled up inside her.

'That's better,' Ben approved. 'It's safe enough to invite me in. I don't bite. Nor do I ravish night sisters— at least not until they've been at the clinic for a little while.'

'I'm glad about that,' Jenny said promptly, knowing that she had lost the fight. She wasn't about to lose the round, however. 'I *would* like a bit of time to myself, though, and I can't possibly get a meal ready with someone cluttering up the flat. There simply isn't enough room,' she rushed on. That wasn't entirely a lie. 'Dinner will be served at seven-thirty, so, like a good guest, please don't arrive early!'

Ben looked startled, as well he might, Jenny thought with some satisfaction. Evidently he wasn't used to being dismissed like that.

'I'll call back at seven thirty-five, ma'am. Thank you!' He waved, then was gone, and Jenny quickly closed the door behind him, not wanting to follow his tall figure with her eyes. From her doorway, she could see halfway along the landing, but she told herself it was silly nonsense to gaze after him like some moon-struck teenager.

It wasn't as if she even fancied him! Anyway—'Think of Lloyd,' she said aloud, compressing her lips tightly as she hurried into the tiny bedroom. Yes, think of Lloyd.

By the time Ben returned, promptly at five minutes past the half-hour, she had showered and changed, trying to make up for her lapse of good manners by dressing as though she were dining out. She took extra pains, too, with her hair. As it was so short, there was little she could do except give it a good brushing, but it was at least clean, and the curling-tongs came in handy. So, too, did the artificial white rose that Brenda, one of her sisters-in-law, had given her for luck.

She surveyed herself in the wardrobe's full-length mirror, not all that pleased with what she saw, but there was nothing more she could do. The shadows under her expressive eyes she had toned down with make-up, but her figure she thought shapeless now, even if Dr Moran did think she had neat ankles! She was too thin, all ankles and joints, as she thought. The dress she wore had been bought just before. . .

Just before you found your fiancé in another woman's arms, she told her reflection. Now it was too loose, but she cinched it in with a wide belt, glad at least that she had a waistline. The dress was a riot of colours in a soft, floaty fabric. There were blues and greys to match her eyes, plus a soft violet running through the pattern. She slipped her feet into high-heeled strappy sandals, then rushed out to the kitchen to prepare the sauce.

The more she thought about it, the more she realised she would have enjoyed an evening out. The sauce was proving recalcitrant and she surveyed it gloomily, wondering why it had developed so many lumps. Then she remembered she hadn't used her perfume spray. Hastily unfastening the voluminous apron, she darted into the bedroom, leaving the sauce to take care of itself.

The doorbell rang just as she was spraying herself sparingly with the jasmine scent she favoured, and she remembered the bolognese. The wretched sauce would be burned and there was nothing else in the flat. She had meant to do the shopping in the morning, and, if she'd been alone, would have made do with a poached egg on toast. Bother Ben the Buccaneer!

Some of the sauce had stuck to the bottom of the pan but Jenny managed to rescue most of it. Then the doorbell rang again, impatiently. Then again and again. He had his finger on the buzzer, and she was determined to give him a piece of her mind. How dared he?

'I'm coming, I'm coming! Wait a minute!' she called through the door. Face flushed and feeling anything but elegant, she eased the door open, prepared to do battle with the impatient Dr Moran.

But it was Lloyd Simmons who stood on the doorstep, his easy smile just as she remembered it.

Jenny gasped, her heart thudding painfully, but she quickly recovered. 'Well, quite a stranger!' she commented, her expression giving nothing away. At least, she hoped it was giving nothing away. Lloyd might be a no-good, two-timing snake, but he didn't lack intelligence. He must know what her feelings would be, seeing him like this, the man who had callously broken her heart, then ground it into the dust for good measure.

She peered past him. 'Are you alone? Or is your wife with you?' she asked pleasantly, and Lloyd smiled, evidently not a bit embarrassed.

'No, she isn't. I'm quite alone, and rather hungry. Something smells good.' Lloyd's smile widened, and he seemed in no doubt that Jenny would invite him in.

He was going to be out of luck! 'I suggest you——' Jenny began, but was interrupted as another figure loomed behind him, a taller man than Lloyd, but leaner, more athletic, a man with an even more deadly charm. Right then, Jenny wished both of them would go to the devil.

CHAPTER FOUR

FOR a moment, Jenny didn't know quite *what* to do. To introduce the two men was going to prove difficult, but Ben solved the problem for her. His dark, enigmatic gaze met hers. 'Shall I call back later, Sister Fraser?' he asked quietly. 'I didn't realise you were expecting company.'

'No, that's quite all right, Doctor,' Jenny said hastily. 'This is Lloyd Simmons—an old friend. My boss, Dr Ben Moran,' she hurried on after a fractional pause, and the two men shook hands.

Jenny's own hands felt anything but steady, but somehow she got a grip on herself. It would never do to let either man know how close she was to hysteria right at this moment. In the circumstances, she thought any woman would have been.

'Would you like to come in?' she asked, her voice under control now, and she stood aside for first Lloyd, then Ben, to enter.

They could not have failed to smell the burned bolognese sauce but neither man commented on it. It was just as well, or she would have given both of them a piece of her mind! It was all Ben the Buccaneer's fault. Perhaps it was unfair to blame him, but if he hadn't had the temerity to invite himself to dinner she could have coped with Lloyd's visit. As it was. . .

'Was there something urgent, Lloyd? A message, perhaps?' Jenny's manner towards him remained cool, and Lloyd turned faintly reproachful eyes upon her, then smiled easily.

He always smiled easily, that charming smile she remembered so well. Then he shrugged, the broad shoulders straining against the expensive cloth of his suit. 'No, it was nothing in particular, Jen. I was in the district, so. . .'

Lloyd favoured dark suits now, Jenny noted. Of course, unlike Ben, he cared about clothes, always wanted to look his best. If clothes mattered to him, so did the knowledge that female heads would turn when they passed him, for he was handsome, fairly tall and always neatly and expensively dressed. His shoes were Gucci—she knew that without even glancing at them. He wouldn't wear ready-mades. Or down-at-heel trainers, she thought, recalling Ben Moran's favourite footwear.

'Would either of you like a drink? There's a Martini, or a soft drink. I'm afraid that's all I can offer—unless you would like a coffee?' Jenny asked hopefully, her eyes going from Lloyd to the doctor, who lounged comfortably in her armchair. Ben looked completely at ease, that little smile hovering about his mouth, his sleepy eyes half closed. Oh, yes, he was going to make himself at home, there was no mistaking that. Well, he was making himself at home in the wrong home!

She almost snapped at her ex-fiancé when he asked hesitantly if he might have coffee. 'If it isn't too much trouble, Jenny, love,' he went on, the endearment grating on her nerves. Of course it had slipped out without Lloyd realising it. She saw that at once, for he nibbled his full lower lip, avoiding her gaze.

'I suppose you can. I'll see to it. Excuse me.' Head held high, she almost stalked into the kitchen to get Ben the bitter lemon he had asked for. Men!

Resentfully, she banged the mug down on its saucer, wishing it was Lloyd's head she was banging against the drainer. Then reason returned and she felt ashamed of her outburst of temper, slight and reasonable though it was. She was supposed to be a psychiatric nurse, a *trained* psychiatric nurse, a ward sister no less, someone

who had her own emotions well in hand. Here she was,
behaving like a child who'd had a promised treat
withdrawn at the last moment. But she had! She
wanted to share her dinner with Ben; there was no
point in trying to deny that. As the meal was hopelessly
burnt, perhaps she ought to be grateful that Lloyd had
turned up when he did.

Eyeing the glutinous mess that was bolognese sauce,
Jenny scraped out what she could then put the sauce-
pan in to soak. The spaghetti, boiled *al dente*, just as
she liked it, was now stone-cold and looked as unap-
petising as the sauce.

All the while she worked in the kitchen she was
wondering what the two men were finding to talk
about, for she could hear the murmur of voices, though
not actual words, and it made her uneasy. What was
Lloyd telling Ben? It was unlikely that he would give
away any secrets, yet. . .

When she returned to the sitting-room with Ben's
ice-cold can of bitter lemon and a cup of coffee for
Lloyd, she found that conversation was still flowing,
Ben obviously exerting himself to put her ex-fiancé at
his ease. And he had succeeded, for Lloyd was in an
expansive mood, waving his hands in the air as he
described a deal to the doctor. He worked in a mer-
chant bank and was destined for high office, everyone
had said so. Somehow that early promise hadn't materialised yet but Jenny felt sure it would, particularly
with a managing wife such as he had now.

'Lloyd was telling me one or two tricks of the trade,'
Ben said lazily, as he got up to prise the can from her
damp hand, their fingers just touching. 'Now I know
how to make money. Lots of it.' He smiled down into
her eyes, and Jenny fought down the urge to smile
back.

Instead she said, 'How interesting for you. I expect
you need extra money. All doctors do.' With hands

that were no longer quite steady, she handed Lloyd his
coffee. 'Here we are. One coffee. Then I shall have to
turn you out, I'm afraid.' Her tone was light but
determined, and Lloyd chuckled, the chuckle she had
thought never to hear again. Yes, in a way she still
loved him, she couldn't deny it. But what hope was
there now?

'I'm sorry, Jen. I seem to have interrupted your
meal. Ben tells me you invited him to dinner
and I——'

'Ben invited himself to dinner,' she corrected him
sweetly, and both men laughed.

'You haven't changed! I was saying to Angie only
yesterday. . .' Lloyd's voice trailed off, and Jenny
waited for him to resume, her nerves taut.

But he didn't. Instead, he busied himself stirring his
coffee, even though he didn't take sugar. Jenny could
feel Ben's intent gaze upon them both. He was assessing them, probing his way gently but inexorably
towards the truth. Yet how could he know? Was it that
obvious to an outsider?

'Is Angie your mother?' Ben asked after a slight
pause, and Jenny flushed with anger. How dared he
bring it out into the open?

'Yes, she is. Lloyd Simmons was my fiancé. Now
he's my stepfather, Doctor. How clever of you to work
that out.' Her voice sounded strained, even to her own
ears, and Lloyd glanced up, the misery in his eyes not
giving her the satisfaction it ought to have done.

'I see,' was all Ben said, but the words he didn't say
hung heavily in the air between the three of them. Why
didn't he say it? He might just as well fill in the gaps.
Why didn't he say, 'You and Lloyd were lovers, then
Mother came on the scene and he married her,
instead'?

If Jenny had met Ben's gaze she would have seen
nothing in it to cause her more resentment. He felt

sympathy for her, but it would have been cruel to show it. Above all, his emotion was one of anger at the way those she loved had treated her. He didn't show that, either. He had suffered enough himself to know exactly how Jenny was feeling at this moment. He judged it time to leave, but he was sure of one thing—he wasn't leaving until her stepfather was safely off the premises.

Ben rose, tall and commanding, his expression bland. 'Since you seem to have burnt the dinner, I guess I'd better make myself a sandwich at home! I think we had better *both* leave Sister Fraser in peace,' he went on, and Lloyd hurriedly got up.

'Yes, it's getting late and I promised I'd ring my wife. She. . .' His voice trailed off, and there was an awkward silence, broken by Jenny.

'Yes, she'll be worrying about you. She always did. I'll say goodnight to you both, then.' She kept her voice level, her gaze indifferent as it rested first upon Lloyd, then on Ben Moran. She felt rather proud of her act but doubted that it fooled Ben. Nothing got past that perceptive gaze. For a moment she hated him. He had slipped past her defences, stripped away the mask she wore so proudly.

His hand rested briefly on her shoulder. 'Goodnight, Sister. Enjoy your rest.' Then he followed Lloyd from the flat, both men talking easily as they walked down the stairs.

Jenny shut the door decisively, then leant against it, her eyes closed. Slowly her thudding heart resumed its normal beat. So, she had seen Lloyd again, a meeting she had both longed for and dreaded. Was it so terrible, after all?

She passed a hand across her eyes, admitting to herself that things could have been worse. That old attraction was still there, but perhaps seeing Lloyd again hadn't been such a bad thing. He was her mother's husband now, and wishing would not undo the past. The love she felt for him would simply have to shrivel up and die.

Rather like the spaghetti bolognese, she thought wryly, as she wandered back into the kitchen and surveyed the remains. It had certainly been some dinner party!

Monday night found Jenny eager to start work. She wasn't as alert as she ought to have been, though, for sleep had eluded her. Instead, she had lain wakeful and watchful, thinking about Lloyd. Thinking about Ben Moran, too, when she ought to have been sleeping and conserving her energy for a hard night on the wards. Psychiatric nursing *was* hard, mentally as well as physically taxing, no matter that many general nurses didn't believe it could be. Being in charge was no sinecure, and Jenny reviewed the tasks she had set herself for this first night.

There might have been patient changes during the weekend, so the first thing would be to acquaint herself with all the patients, more especially any new ones. After hand-over, she decided, she would do just that. Then get to know the ward staff, listen to them, for that was important, too. Sometimes one got so involved with the patients and their problems that one forgot the nurses also had problems, difficulties that they needed to talk over with someone senior. Yes, it was good to be back on duty. That way left her no time to brood, to recall the good times, to think wistfully of what might have been.

'Ah, good, good! You are early!' Sister Astley's delightfully accented voice greeted her, and Jenny felt better. This was where she belonged. Damn Lloyd Simmons! She didn't need him—she didn't need *any* man.

'The new girl likes to appear keen,' she said solemnly, and Resi Astley giggled.

'We have two new admissions since Friday, both ladies of a certain age,' the sister went on, ushering Jenny into the spacious ward office. There were two nurses there already.

'Ah, here we have our staff nurse, Beryl Templar, and Lesley Bell, who is a nursing aide. This is our new night sister, Jenny Fraser,' Resi said.

Staff Nurse Templar was in her thirties, a tall red-head with a pleasant freckled face and an engaging smile. Jenny took to her straight away. Lesley Bell was a plump girl, nearly twenty-one, filling in time until she began her nurse training.

'I wasn't sure what I wanted to do, Sister,' she began hesitantly. 'I know you'll think I ought to have done by now, though.'

'I think nothing of the sort,' Jenny said kindly. 'Sometimes we need a period of reflection before we really know *what* we want from life. If you've had work experience, then you've got something extra to bring to psychiatric nursing and that must be good.'

The girl flushed, obviously pleased, and Jenny wondered whether anyone had been making snide remarks. Plenty of people took to psychiatric nursing later, and it was no disgrace to try different jobs first. She decided she must keep an eye on the girl, see how she shaped up, encourage her—or discourage her, as the case might be.

'Now, tell me the worst,' she invited, and Sister Astley waved her hands expressively.

'Tonight we are here together. Then, my friend, you're on your own! This Mrs Lawrence you saw last week. She's a problem.' Sister Astley frowned, and Jenny's heart sank. She'd had that feeling. Mrs Lawrence presumably didn't fit into the ward.

And that proved to be the case. After the rest of the night shift had turned up, Jenny accompanied Resi Astley on her rounds.

'I think we ought to begin with Mrs Lawrence, if you don't mind?' Jenny suggested. 'I do at least know her, and it won't seem odd if I seek her out first.'

Resi shrugged. 'If you wish, then of course you must, but I'll be in the TV-room. Mrs Lawrence and I do not have a good relationship, and you may be just what she needs, eh?'

I doubt that, Jenny thought grimly, but at least she must try. She found Mrs Lawrence in bed, even though it was barely nine o'clock. The room was a four-bedder, and apparently that was one of the patient's grumbles. She had wanted—no, *insisted* upon having a single room, but, bearing in mind Marie Thomson's words on her first day, Jenny knew that wouldn't have been allowed. Persuading Mrs Lawrence of that might be difficult, though.

'Hello, Mrs Lawrence,' she began carefully. 'Perhaps you don't recognise me in uniform? We all look different in mufti,' she went on, as the woman gazed at her blankly. 'I'm Jenny Fraser, the new night sister. We met when Dr Moran interviewed you.'

'Oh, did we? Oh, yes, I think I remember—you wore that pretty lavender suit, didn't you? Come and sit down, Sister. I've had no one to talk to and I'm utterly bored!' Mrs Lawrence got out of bed, reaching for a pretty silk dressing-gown.

'What about your neighbours in the other beds? Aren't they friendly?' Jenny asked casually, once the patient was comfortably seated in an armchair over by the window. The room was large, with plenty of space between the beds, and each could be made more private if the bed curtains were drawn. Though for someone used to privacy Jenny could see that it wasn't ideal. Would it be so bad if Mrs Lawrence was given a room on her own? She didn't appear to be suicidal, far from it, and Jenny made a mental note to see what could be done.

'Oh, them!' Mrs Lawrence waved a hand, effectively dismissing her fellow patients. 'They're such dreadful people, Sister, you can have no idea. Some of them are *mad*, I'm sure of it!'

Jenny bent her head to consult her list of patients. 'I doubt that, Mrs Lawrence. We try to keep patients with similar problems together. They wouldn't give you a room with anyone suffering from a serious disorder, like schizophrenia. Who have you got in here? Um— there's Mrs Manderley, Miss Millington, the new lady, and Mrs Durrant. They are more or less in your age-group, you know, and——'

'But they're *ill*! Dr Moran himself said I wasn't ill, I just needed rest, away from the pressures of life. I'm not ill, Sister!' Mrs Lawrence was getting agitated, and abruptly she got up and began pacing up and down the room.

'No one has suggested you are,' Jenny said soothingly, 'and if you really can't stay in this room, perhaps we may be able to move you. I'll have to check with Sister Astley—I'm the new girl, after all. I can't start making sweeping changes,' she pointed out calmly. 'Do you feel any better for your two days in the clinic?'

There was a low shuddering sigh from the patient, then she shook her head. 'No, not really. I think it was all a dreadful mistake. Perhaps I ought to discharge myself. But that wouldn't be allowed, would it?' She stopped her perambulating and came and stood beside Jenny.

'Why not? There's nothing to stop you discharging yourself. You're free to leave whenever you wish, but it would be a pity. Dr Moran will be upset, I should imagine,' Jenny went on, her expressive eyes fixed upon the patient's face.

'Yes, Dr Moran. Ben the Buccaneer—that's what they call him, you know.' The glimmer of a smile lit the woman's face. 'He's very good-looking, isn't he? Yes, I suppose *he* would be disappointed.'

'Perhaps you could give the clinic a trial for a few days? A week, say, then discuss a move with Dr Moran or the day sister. You can't really expect to feel better after only two days. You need the rest, I think—so does Dr Moran,' Jenny said carefully, aware that whatever Dr Moran thought was best would be likely to weigh heavily with this particular patient. Perhaps he wouldn't appreciate her making use of his influence in this way, but it was all for the patient's good.

'Yes, I'll do that,' Mrs Lawrence agreed slowly. 'But I'm not really ill, am I? Not like that poor Sophie? I feel sorry for her. She came over to speak to me after supper and at first I didn't know what to say to her. I was afraid, to tell the truth,' Mrs Lawrence admitted. 'She has a habit of sitting screaming at times and I'm sure she hears voices, but she isn't violent. Quite the reverse. I like her.' She began plucking at the cord tying her dressing-gown. 'Thank God I've never been like that!'

'I think we all thank Him for that, Mrs Lawrence. Sophie lives in her own little world part of the time, and it's up to all of us to help her. Any help you *can* give in the short while you're with us would be appreciated, I'm sure.' Sometimes that was therapeutic in itself, and, even if it didn't actually help, it took people's minds off their own particular problems, helped them to see that they weren't the only ones who were suffering.

'And try to get on with your bed-neighbours if you can,' Jenny advised, as she rose to leave. 'I must get on and speak to every patient before they all troop off to bed, but I'll be back in here later on. And you know where the night office is if you want to come in to have a chat.'

'Do you suppose Dr Moran will be around tonight?'

Mrs Lawrence's voice arrested Jenny as she was about to get on with the round.

'I've no idea. Does he work at night, then?' The thought simply hadn't occurred to her. Oh, no! Surely she wasn't to have him troubling her thoughts on night duty as well!

'He was here last night. I wonder what sort of home life he has?' Mrs Lawrence's words echoed Jenny's own thoughts. 'He's such a caring man, he ought to have a caring wife. Are you married, Sister?'

Caught off balance, Jenny stared for a moment, then shook her head. 'No, I'm heart-whole and fancy-free, but I'm afraid I can't provide a home life for Dr Moran!'

'Well, now, that's a pity, Sister Fraser,' an amused voice said, and Ben Moran himself strolled into the room, his smile lighting up the dimly lit bedroom. Jenny found herself flushing, and saw the way his eyes narrowed. Damn the man!

'Mrs Lawrence was saying you ought to have a caring wife, Doctor, and I was just pointing out that I wouldn't fulfil any of the reqirements,' she said hastily, and Ben chuckled.

'Why, thank you, Mrs Lawrence,' he said, making her a bow. The woman giggled, a pleasantly girlish sound that Jenny wouldn't have thought her capable of making. 'I doubt if Sister Fraser and I could agree for five minutes. That's a pity, isn't it, Sister?'

That mocking smile was back again, and Jenny bitterly resented the way he baited her. Wasn't knowing her secret sorrow enough for him? Did he have to torment her every hour of the day and night? But he didn't, he didn't! It was all in her mind!

She turned to go, but to her consternation Ben quickly said goodnight to the patient, and followed her out. 'Mustn't stay unchaperoned, Sister! Have you forgotten already?' he chided gently.

'I'm sorry I forgot, Dr Ben,' Jenny said with mock sweetness.

Then Ben moved nearer, and Jenny fought down the urge to turn and run. 'There's something *I* keep forgetting,' he went on, in the same quiet tone, and a surprised Jenny opened her mouth to ask him what it was. But she remained silent after all, her lips still parted, the expression in his eyes preventing her from speaking. Her breathing was irregular, and the nurse in her diagnosed tension as a possible cause. Then Ben's lips met hers and all thoughts of nursing vanished from her mind.

The kiss was gentle, tentative, almost as if Ben hadn't kissed anyone for a very long time and wasn't sure he could remember how it was done. Then his strong arms tightened about her, one large hand moulding her body to his, and Jenny knew him for no amateur. This was the touch of an expert!

Belatedly she began to struggle, aware that she was enjoying the kiss and that it must, therefore, be wrong. She was being disloyal to Lloyd's memory. Lloyd was still the man she yearned for, no matter that he was now out of reach. She loved him, so she couldn't possibly enjoy another man's kiss. Or so she told herself.

Reluctantly, Ben let her go, wondering what had come over him. Dismissing it as a temporary spring madness was about all he could do, yet. . .

'I spent all last week wondering whether your mouth was as kissable as it looked,' he admitted bluntly. Then, before Jenny could find her tongue, he hurried away, disappearing into the room at the end of the corridor. The fire door closed behind him, and she was left standing outside the bedroom, wishing she had the right to follow him.

Wonderingly, she pressed a hand against her lips, scarcely believing that Ben had wanted to kiss her. It did wonders for her self-esteem, but it was a dazed and shaken night sister who continued her rounds of the patients. She felt they were getting only half a sister. The other half was following Ben the Buccaneer.

CHAPTER FIVE

To JENNY'S consternation, Ben Moran reappeared later and seemed set to spend what remained of the night in the clinic. Did he have a home life? she wondered, as she sat in the night office studying some of the case-notes. Surely he had a home—and a wife— to go to?

Being a sensible girl, she had dismissed his kiss as nothing more than an experiment. She took at face value his explanation that he wanted to see if she was as kissable as she looked. Well, he knew the answer now!

It had been thoughtless of him to take her unawares, though, and, try as she might to find excuses for his behaviour, Jenny couldn't help feeling disappointed in him. Still. . . She shrugged away the niggling feeling, still wondering why he was here at all. There was, as far as she could see, no earthly reason why a consultant psychiatrist should come on night duty, almost as if he didn't want to be alone. If there was trouble brewing, the duty doctor and trained nursing staff could be expected to cope with it. The art of psychiatric nursing was to spot trouble *before* it began to brew.

Jenny's lips curved into a smile. She had to admit that having Ben on the ward gave her a pleasant feeling of security and well-being, no matter what. He——

A faint sound from outside the office caused her to glance up, and she almost expected to see the man himself lounging in the doorway, smile at the ready. But there was no one. Yet she had heard something, she knew it. With psychiatric patients one had to be alert.

Hastily she got up then peered out into the darkened corridor. The corridor was empty yet someone *had* passed the door. It could have been one of the nursing aides but Jenny didn't think so.

The remainder of the staff were sitting in the television-room with one or two patients who remained up, the staff nurse being on duty at the other end of the unit. The nursing aides and student were supposed to divide their time between the two sections, but as it was quiet Jenny had allowed them to watch a particularly good film on TV. Sister Astley had gone for her supper-break, and Jenny was at a loss, not knowing the patients well and thinking that perhaps she had imagined the silent passer-by. Yet, after Ben had kissed her and she had wandered miserably back to the office, she'd had the sensation of being watched. And where was Ben now?

There was only one way to reassure herself that all was well, and that was to make a full round. Taking her torch and locking the office door behind her, Jenny patted the comforting presence of her alarm which lay snugly in her pocket.

Unable to shake off that vague feeling of unease, she hurried up the short, winding staircase that led to the main sleeping area—a former master bedroom, where six patients slept. One of these was Sophie Clary, and Jenny had a hunch the girl would be missing. But she was mistaken. Sophie was in her bed, tossing restlessly to be sure, but unmistakably there. Four of the other beds were occupied, the remaining one being vacant. No problem there, then.

The clinic didn't have an admission ward as such, newcomers being integrated straight away, a principle Jenny thoroughly agreed with. Shining the torch on her list, she checked the newcomers: Mrs Lawrence was down the stairs in the room to the right of the office, so was Miss Millington. Well, she would check on those first as well as the two women who shared that room, before setting off to seek out someone who might become a problem—Anne Bomford.

Mrs Lawrence was awake, and Jenny noted in surprise that she and Miss Millington were holding a whispered conversation.

'Is everything all right, ladies?' Jenny asked softly, and Miss Millington raised a hand in acknowledgment.

'Yes, thank you, Sister. I hope we aren't disturbing anyone?' Mrs Lawrence said, and Jenny shook her head.

'No, that's fine. I'm just counting heads!' Noting that the other two occupants of the room were safely in bed, Jenny left, her shoes making no sound on the thickly carpeted floors. Now for Anne Bomford.

Anne wasn't where she should have been, but Jenny recalled seeing her in the TV-room. As she was about to go into the room, Lesley Bell came bustling up.

'Were you looking for me, Sister? I've just done a quick head-count in the other wing. All present and correct,' she announced, beaming at Jenny, who frowned.

'Is everyone accounted for, then? I thought—no, I'm *sure* someone passed the office door but when I got up to look, I couldn't see anyone. Where's Anne Bomford?'

Lesley looked surprised. 'Why, she's in bed, Sister. I saw her go in there not half an hour ago. She got bored with the TV and——'

Without waiting for any more, Jenny went swiftly into the TV-room and scanned the occupants. Several heads turned towards her and she indicated the TV. 'Could you turn it down a bit, please? Where's Anne Bomford?'

The student nurse switched the sound off and hastily got up, her face red. 'She went to bed, Sister.'

'She isn't there now and the bed hasn't been touched. Can you look for her, please?' Jenny said crisply, annoyed with herself more than with the junior staff, though they knew the patient better than she did, and ought to have been wary. Still, it couldn't be helped. What was done was done.

Deciding against returning to the office, Jenny quickly checked the remainder of the patients. The two who had been in the television-room were making tea in the small ward kitchen.

'Like a cuppa, Sister?' Dorothy Hurley asked. 'I'm going home tomorrow and I don't want to go to bed tonight. Thought I'd stay up—if that's all right?'

'It's fine by me, but have you had your night medication? No, you don't have any now, do you?' Jenny's memory was excellent and she knew exactly who had sleeping medicine and who didn't. 'Stay up by all means and yes, I'd love a cup. I'll join you in the kitchen shortly. I must look for Anne Bomford. Have you any idea where she might be?'

'Well, I shouldn't say. . .' Mrs Hurley began hesitantly. 'She spends too much time following the doctor around and he'll be doing a round soon. I shouldn't wonder if she wasn't hanging about looking for him. She might be in the grounds, even.'

'But the doors are locked! At least they're locked after dark,' Jenny pointed out, and Mrs Hurley put a finger against her nose.

'Ah, but Anne finds ways, Sister, she finds ways! Anyhow, I'll just boil the kettle again.' She disappeared into the kitchen, leaving Jenny coldly angry.

So, Anne Bomford was another of Ben the Buccaneer's conquest's, was she? He had no right to encourage her in some silly hero-worship! Men were all alike, they——

No, she mustn't brand everyone a snake in the grass like Lloyd. Anyway, it was unfair to snakes! Jenny's sense of humour came to her rescue, and she was able to view the whole matter more objectively. Ben couldn't help his fatal attraction, and Anne was an immature, impressionable young woman.

The impressionable young woman was nowhere to be found in the whole of the acute floor and Jenny widened the search to include the lower floors. Resi Astley had by this time returned from her break.

'It isn't like Anne to wander off,' she commented when Jenny put her in the picture. 'She *might* have gone for a walk in the grounds, perhaps, but it's raining, and I didn't say she could go out. Has Dr——? Ah, Ben!'

Jenny whirled round, to come face to face with Ben Moran. Behind him trailed the tall, forlorn figure of Anne Bomford.

Barely acknowledging the psychiatrist, Jenny spoke directly to the patient. 'We were worried about you, Anne. At least *I* was! As I'm new, I didn't realise you went for nocturnal walks. You're wet!'

Anne's eyes glinted, and Jenny wasn't sure whether she was amused or angry. With Anne it was difficult to be sure. 'I went for a little stroll and met Dr Ben. Sorry, Sister. If I'd known you were worried, I would have told you. But then you might have told me I couldn't go out, mightn't you?' she added, and Jenny smiled, despite her annoyance.

'Well, yes, I might have done,' she conceded. 'But I would have checked first with Sister Astley. You'll catch your death of cold—have a warm-up in the kitchen. They're making tea in there.'

Anne glanced down in apparent surprise at her muddy slippers and the wet hem of her flowered nightie. 'Yes, it is a bit damp out. I could do with some tea.' She smiled her charming smile at Jenny, who wasn't fooled for an instant.

'It was a good job I heard you pass the office door,' Jenny commented, and Anne turned back, her big round face wearing a puzzled expression.

'I didn't pass *your* door, Sister. I went the other way. There's another door upstairs leading to the gallery. I crossed that then went down the back stairs.'

'But I heard you! At least, I thought I heard someone,' Jenny said half to herself. 'Never mind, Lesley will get you some dry clothes. We could do with the rain, anyway.'

'Mm, I've been given a patch of garden around the back of the clinic. See you!' With a cheery wave, Anne followed Sister Astley, leaving Jenny alone with Dr Moran.

'I'm glad you found Anne, Doctor,' she said levelly. 'I heard that she follows you around and I suppose she was looking for you as usual?' Try as she might, Jenny couldn't keep the edge out of her voice, and Ben raised a heavy brow then smiled his lazy smile.

'Where did you get the idea that Anne follows me around? It was only by chance I——'

'I'm sure we can at least be honest with each other, Doctor!' Jenny said tightly, her eyes sparking at him. 'Someone said Anne followed you around, and this— this person thought the girl was probably lying in wait for you. I realise you're a victim of your own charm. You admitted as much yourself, but surely you could discourage her? I was worried in case she ran away. No one told me she's allowed out at nights!'

When Ben made no answer, merely stood surveying her thoughtfully, Jenny hurried on, 'I know that because I'm new I can't be expected to understand everything that goes on, but I would have thought——'

'And I would have thought you might have checked your facts, Jenny.' Ben's words of reproof were mild enough and he was still smiling, and this fuelled Jenny's anger. So, he thought it was amusing, did he? The patient might have wandered off and been run over or raped or something, and here he was, smiling!

'I'm sorry,' she said stiffly. 'Perhaps I ought not to

take you to task, but at night the patients are *my* responsibility and I hope you *will* discourage Anne Bomford from hanging around after you! My task is difficult enough. Excuse me.'

Mentally counting to twenty, Jenny turned her back on the maddeningly attractive psychiatrist, and went in search of the patient herself. Let Dr Moran think what he wanted about her; her first duty was to the patients and she would have been neglecting that duty if she hadn't asked him to mend his ways.

Of course, she reflected, she had a colossal cheek to tell the head of the clinic how he should go about his business. After all, they were *his* patients as well, and once she had cooled down and put the image of Lloyd Simmons from her mind, Jenny realised that. Sipping a cup of nearly scalding tea in the tiny kitchen a little later, she mulled over what she had said. She was at fault, she couldn't deny it. But there was something about Ben Moran that brought out the fiery, argumentative side of her nature. He had said she couldn't be called 'Fraser the Feminist', but little did he know that she had often been called 'Fraser the Fiery'!

Anne had drifted away, leaving her dirty cup and saucer on the draining board, and Jenny hadn't the heart to call her back and remind her of the rule that patients washed up their own crockery after making tea or snacks. Tonight wasn't the time for a confrontation—the one with the psychiatrist had been enough to last all week. She felt desperately tired, drained, and this was only her first night. What she would be like by the end of the week, she didn't know. One thing was for sure—she would keep well out of the way of Dr Ben Moran!

She decided against taking a proper break when her suppertime came around, instead sending down for one of the juniors to buy her a sandwich. A cup of tea from

the ward kitchen and a sandwich would keep her going
until seven, when the shifts changed.

Unlike general hospitals, the clinic ran only straight
shifts and there were no split duties as a rule. The day
shift began at seven, with the night staff leaving at
seven-thirty, the half-hour overlap being beneficial to
patients as well as staff. Jenny determined to ask her
day counterpart a little about Anne Bomford. On day
duty, she had hardly seen the girl, who helped in the
psycho-geriatric wing on the ground floor. Yes, Anne
could be a problem at nights—particularly with a new
and untried night sister.

Jenny bit into her cheese and pickle sandwich,
wishing she had chosen something else. Visions of the
spaghetti she had so nearly served to the psychiatrist
hovered before her, and she chuckled. What wouldn't
she give for a decent meal right now! Night duty always
set her taste-buds working overtime, at least on quiet
nights, and——

'I wish I could join in the joke,' a softly seductive
voice spoke almost in her ear, and Jenny jumped up,
knocking the telephone to one side in her agitation.

'Oh, it's you! I didn't hear you. I'm sorry,' she said
hastily, as Ben Moran strolled into her office. 'I was
miles away—thinking about food, actually,' she added.

'I think about food a lot on nights,' Ben admitted,
leaning against the filing cabinet and surveying her
from under half-closed black lashes. 'Like spaghetti
bolognese, for instance,' he went on conversationally,
and Jenny went scarlet. He would mention that!

'Yes, like spaghetti with bolognese sauce stuck to
the bottom of the pan,' she agreed, and he chuckled.

'Is that what happened? That's too bad. We must do
something about that. How about dining with me one
day? I'm no hand at cooking but I could open a few
packets.' His lazy smile warmed her and for a moment
Jenny was tempted, but she sternly resisted temptation.

No good would come of it, no good at all. Remember Lloyd.

'Thank you, Doctor, but I don't——'

'What's with this Doctor this and Doctor that?' he demanded, straightening a little. 'I thought I was Ben?'

'Yes, of course. Ben the Buccaneer,' Jenny said deliberately, her eyes on his face, and he nodded, that little slick of hair falling over one eye, making him indeed look like a pirate from days gone by, ready to do a bit of swashbuckling. Well, he needn't buckle his swash anywhere near *her*!

'Do I figure at all in your inner arguments, Sister Fraser?' Ben asked, eyeing her with interest. He wished he knew what went on in his new sister's neat little mind. He would have liked to get to know her better, but. . . It wouldn't do. He ought to apologise for kissing her, he supposed, but knew he wouldn't. Why apologise for an interlude they had both enjoyed?

'Sometimes,' Jenny admitted. 'I owe you an apology, anyway. I shouldn't have said what I did about Anne Bomford, but I still think I was in the right, Doc—Ben,' she amended hastily. 'If she follows you around, you——'

Ben held up a large hand, then resumed his casual stance by the filing cabinet. 'Let's get one thing clear, then we can begin again. Anne doesn't follow *me* around, she follows Dr Walter. You've met him, haven't you?'

At Jenny's surprised nod, he went on, 'So—he's young and handsome, and personable, I guess you would call it. He's also happily married. Don't get me wrong, but he has a caring nature—too caring, perhaps, and patients like Anne Bomford take advantage of him. He's supposed to be on duty tonight but I came instead. Anne was hanging around waiting for him, but she came across me instead, so she's one disappointed lady!'

'I can't think why!' Jenny exclaimed, before she thought better of it. 'You're personable and—and good-looking, and seem to be quite a hit with the other ladies. She might prefer you. She——' Her voice died away and she cursed her unruly tongue. How much she had given away she wasn't sure, but it might have been too much. She had handed Ben a weapon he could use against her, and she felt terribly vulnerable.

'Thank you for the high praise, Sister Fraser.' There was laughter in Ben's eyes, and Jenny smiled. 'That's better. You don't look so severe when you smile. You'll have to do it more often,' he commented.

'Do I look severe? No one has ever told me that!' Surely she didn't. Of course, with her plain hairstyle and her determined, stubborn chin in full view, she *might* sometimes look less than easygoing, but severe—never! 'I don't! I'm sure I don't. Anyway, do you want to tell me anything about Anne?' Jenny hurried on.

Ben shrugged. 'What is there to tell about her? I've already told you I dislike labelling people and——'

'It *does* help sometimes,' Jenny insisted, rising to her feet and crumpling up the Cellophane wrapping of her sandwich. 'I rather wish the night canteen had more variety in sandwiches, Ben. Perhaps you could drop a word in someone's ear?' she suggested, tilting her head to one side as she surveyed him. He looked tired. She hadn't noticed it before. No, she told herself, you were too wrapped up in your own problems, you forgot that Ben might have problems, too. 'You look tired,' she said aloud.

'Does that thought follow on from the complaint about the sandwiches? *I* don't sit up half the night making them!'

Jenny bit her lip, then her smile broadened. 'You might. How am I to know? Anyway, you don't want to talk about Anne—what do you want to talk about?'

Ben made a show of glancing at his watch. Three twenty-five on a Tuesday morning. *The* Tuesday morning—Louise's birthday. Pain showed briefly in his eyes. 'Nothing in particular, but next time I prepare the sandwiches I'll bear your request in mind! Goodnight, Sister!' He raised a hand in farewell, then changed his mind. 'How about dinner this evening?'

'Cheese sandwiches?' Jenny suggested wickedly, and he grinned down at her.

'Perhaps. Do you sleep first then tackle the day's chores, or sleep later?'

'Sleep first. I shall go straight back to my flat, change then fall into bed,' Jenny said firmly. 'It works better that way. I can't sleep if I potter about first. I'm usually up again about two in the afternoon, then I stay up.'

'Fine. Let's say six-thirty?' he suggested. 'There's a little restaurant I know and their food is out of this world. It isn't frequented by hospital folk, either, so we can relax, get away from patient problems. I'll pick you up at your flat. See you!'

Without waiting for Jenny's acquiescence or otherwise, Ben was gone, leaving the office emptier than before, and a curious void in Jenny's heart. Then resistance set in. The man had a nerve, assuming she would calmly put aside whatever she had planned for the early evening, just so she could wine and dine with Ben the Buccaneer!

She had to acknowledge much later, as she and Resi prepared to hand over to the day sister, that she hadn't actually planned anything for the day, so she didn't have any real excuse for refusing his invitation! In fact, she was looking forward to it.

Daylight brought rain, great amounts of it, and a grey, leaden sky. It also brought Rachel Bonner, who almost pranced into the office, full of the joys of spring, Jenny thought sourly. Her own eyelids felt heavy, too heavy to stay open, but that wasn't unusual, since she hadn't slept much lately. She must drive straight home and fall into bed before fatigue overcame her.

'Hello, Rachel,' Jenny greeted her quietly. 'It's been an uneventful night—except for Anne Bomford. She took a stroll in the rain but she's sleeping now.'

Rachel's smile was brief, and she set her case down on a chair without glancing at Jenny. 'If I know Anne, she'll be the devil to wake this morning and I particularly wanted to have a talk with her. She hates getting up in the morning. It's going to be a busy day and I have to go home early. My in-laws chose this week to go on holiday and I've got to have the children.'

'Children?' Jenny echoed blankly. 'I'm sorry, I didn't know you were married. How old are they?' Having children, presumably young ones, might go some way to excusing Rachel's air of abstraction, her sometimes short fuse.

'Mm? Oh, I'm divorced. Tim's twelve and Jane's nearly nine. They aren't any real bother, but I'd rather not have them this week. It meant I had to cancel a date tonight, but never mind.' Rachel continued to take folders out of her case and Jenny watched without actually seeing her.

Rachel had to break a date for tonight! It might just be a coincidence, but she didn't think so. Because Rachel couldn't come out tonight, Ben had decided that Sister Fraser would make a suitable substitute. Well, she wouldn't!

Anger vied with hurt pride in Jenny's mind as she handed over to Marie Thomson. Anger, hurt pride, and something more—a deep, deep ache in her heart. No one liked being second best and she had been foolish enough to read more into the dinner invitation than Ben had intended. If she felt let down now, it was no-one's fault but her own. But it hurt. It hurt more than he must ever know.

CHAPTER SIX

PRIDE came to Jenny's rescue, and she was ready well before six-thirty that evening. There was, she told her mirror firmly, no reason why she shouldn't dine with Ben. And, despite Rachel Bonner, she was looking forward to dining out with a handsome man. Before Lloyd, there hadn't been anyone special. Oh, she had enjoyed a few casual friendships, been wined and dined, escorted to the cinema or the theatre. But they had been just that—friendships, strictly platonic. Only to Lloyd had she given her heart, her love. She sighed, noting the dark smudges under her eyes.

Then, turning deliberately away from her reflection, she hurried to close the windows, not wanting to keep Ben the Buccaneer waiting.

Ben cast an admiring glance her way when he arrived a few minutes later. His smile warmed her, but Jenny tried not to let it unsettle her. He was simply being a psychiatrist, a caring, understanding man. A caring, understanding man who wanted an hour or two off duty to relax, away from the pressures of his exacting work. Well, *she* wouldn't be doing any pressurising.

'I like that outfit,' he commented as they emerged into the spring evening. The air felt fresh and clean after the earlier rain, though it was still cold, and Jenny was glad of her warm suit, in a pale heather shade. After some thought, she had teamed it with a crisp white blouse and a black velvet bow-tie.

Her eyes glowed as she thanked him prettily. 'A somewhat tame compliment,' she couldn't resist adding, 'but thank you, anyway!'

Ben's lips quivered and there was a gleam in those dark eyes that made Jenny catch her breath suddenly.

'The place we're going to is called the Artful Pheasant, believe it or not,' he said as he started the car.

'That sounds promising! Whereabouts is it?'

'It's very much a local favourite,' Ben told her. 'The day-trippers haven't found it yet. It's the other side of Eastbourne, in a little hamlet called Hangley Cross. Do you know it?' he asked, turning right into a narrow, high-banked lane.

Puzzled, Jenny shook her head. 'No, I've never heard of Hangley Cross. Oh—is there a windmill there?'

'Mm, about a mile outside the village. It's dilapidated, though, probably beyond restoration. I like windmills,' he added, surprisingly, and Jenny nodded in agreement, glad they could stay away from contentious subjects.

'Yes, so do I. And Martello towers, too. It's my ambition to live in a Martello tower!' she admitted. 'It's only a pipe-dream but people *do* convert them into comfortable homes.'

'That's right. And how about an abandoned lighthouse? I always wanted—damn!' Ben braked sharply, and Jenny glanced about her in dismay. Rachel Bonner's distinctive sports car had just cut out in front of them from a side-road. Was she, too, dining at the Artful Pheasant? Jenny wondered.

'It looks as if Rachel could make it, after all,' she commented lightly, determined to let Ben know that she realised he should have been escorting the therapist. 'I wonder where the children are?'

Ben frowned. 'She's probably left them on their own. It wouldn't be the first time, but——' He bit back whatever he had been about to say, while Jenny struggled with her disappointment that she wasn't to have Ben to herself. She tried to feel charitable towards Rachel, and eventually managed it, but it wasn't easy.

'Perhaps we shall be dining *à trois*?' she suggested.

'Yes, I have the feeling we will be.' Ben's tone was dry, and he sounded less than pleased at the idea.

They completed the drive in a kind of waiting silence, but Rachel's car was no longer in front of them as they drew up outside the restaurant, and Jenny relaxed. Probably Rachel had been on her way to pick up the children.

The Artful Pheasant proved to be a country-club-style restaurant, and Jenny wished she had dressed up more. Her suit was good, but she felt it was too countrified for the smart atmosphere. Ben was wearing a dark suit and actually sported a necktie, something which evidently annoyed him, for immediately they were shown to their reserved table he loosened the tie and heaved a sigh of relief.

Jenny chuckled. 'It's a pity you couldn't wear your jumble sale outfit in here!'

'Now that remark hurt! I get my clothes from charity shops, not jumble sales!' he riposted, then leaned back, so obviously at his ease that Jenny envied him. Their eyes met, and hastily she began to peruse the menu.

They both chose the same meal—a prawn cocktail starter followed by chicken *à la roi*, with mountains of fresh vegetables. Jenny approved the sharp, tangy white wine he had chosen to go with the meal, and glanced up to tell him so, but that little mocking smile was on his lips again, so she busied herself breaking her roll.

'Everything to your satisfaction, Sister?' he asked softly, and, bright-eyed, Jenny nodded.

'Lovely, Doctor. Really lovely,' she assured him, wondering whether his smile mocked her or himself. He was an enigma. 'You're an enigma, you know,' she said slowly.

'*Am* I? Why?' Ben still seemed amused. 'Here you
see a perfectly ordinary bloke. One who——' Here
Jenny snorted in disbelief, and he chuckled.

'All right. So I'm not perfectly ordinary. Who wants
to be ordinary, anyway? Here I am, a tall, maddeningly
attractive shrink with a perfectly ordinary lifestyle, and
you say I'm an enigma. How come?' White teeth
gleamed in the darkly handsome buccaneer's face, and
Jenny nibbled her lip, wondering what she had started.
At least he wasn't like Lloyd, taking himself so
seriously that a light, verbal sparring match was out of
the question. Oh, damn Lloyd!

'You come on duty at night, when everyone knows
consultants keep regular hours,' she ventured, not
wanting him to think she was prying. 'Then you disap-
pear, only to reappear later on, like—like some restless
spirit from times past. Oh—and why is Easterwood
such a hotch-potch of periods?' she added, thinking of
times past. 'I keep meaning to ask someone but there
never seems the time.'

'About appearing and reappearing. . .' He hesitated
for a moment. 'I live just down the road. There are a
few big houses in Southdown Road, about a mile from
the main gates. You know them?'

'No, I come round by the Red Lion. It's a short cut.'
Tonight, she decided silently, she would take a detour
and discover Southdown Road for herself.

'So—I can get to Easterwood within a few minutes,
if there's an emergency. As to why I come on nights at
all. . .' Ben let the sentence trail off for a moment. It
was still Tuesday, still Louise's birthday. 'I live alone
and I get lonely. Does that answer your question?'

Jenny knew quite well he didn't live alone, but she
smiled, accepting graciously that she wasn't to be told
any more. She hadn't forgotten that telephone call he'd
had on her first day at the clinic.

'You haven't answered my other question, though.

The neo-Georgian exterior and the remains of a medieval great hall inside. Why, please?' she asked meekly, and Ben seemed to relax. Her observant eye had seen the way he held his wine glass while talking about himself. His fingers had tightened on the stem of the glass, no matter that he appeared perfectly at his ease. There was some mystery there, something that hurt him, and Jenny had the absurd desire to urge him to confide in her. She wanted desperately to help him, offer succour, wipe away the unshed tears as she might do to a child, or a patient.

It was stupid, for Ben was neither. Yet she sensed that he needed to confide in someone, needed a soft, cool hand on his brow, a comforting arm about his shoulders. Without being consciously aware of it, she put out her small hand and covered his. She found herself patting it comfortingly. Then, when she realised what she was doing, she hastily snatched her hand away, her face flaming.

Ben's slow smile widened. 'A little TLC?' he asked, and, still pink, Jenny nodded.

'I'm sorry. I can't seem to leave nursing behind me!' She only hoped he would accept her poor excuse.

'I rather enjoyed it,' he admitted. 'As to the fake Georgian exterior, Easterwood was built at the turn of the century. The owner liked Georgian style, I believe,' he went on, and Jenny noticed a faint note of constraint in his voice. 'He was rather an eccentric. And a collector. That explains the odds and ends of furniture. He had more money than sense, but the patients seem to approve.'

'Everything blends in well,' Jenny assured him. 'I particularly like the spaciousness of the rooms, too. I——' She stopped. She had been about to ask why more patients couldn't have single rooms, but this wasn't the time or place. Ben needed to get away from work.

'Keep going,' he encouraged. 'I like to hear you talk.'

'Do you? Why?' Jenny's lips had parted involuntarily, and Ben thought how very desirable she looked just then. Yes, her mouth *was* kissable.

'You have a faint Scots lilt in your voice. It's still there, but you mayn't be aware of it,' he told her, his own voice harsh with the emotion he had to suppress.

'Like your faint Australian lilt,' she countered. 'Though *that's* overlaid with some other accent. American, I think. Yes, definitely American,' she said firmly.

'I've been around. I'm a citizen of the world,' he said, then raised his glass. 'Let's drink a toast: to a long and happy stay at Easterwood for Sister Jenny Fraser!'

Jenny clinked her glass against his, and it was inevitable that their fingers should touch. She carefully avoided his eyes, afraid that her own would reveal too much. Why, she wondered, do I feel so at ease with him, a man I scarcely know?

'Now,' Ben said decisively. 'It's my turn to ask a question. What brought you to Sussex, in particular?'

Jenny considered, turning her glass round and round. 'I suppose I could have stayed in London, despite. . . everything, but I saw this job advertised and it seemed to be just what I wanted. A job I'd been waiting for,' she went on, surprised. Yes, that was it. 'It was as if I *had* to come to the Easterwood,' she said reflectively. 'I need the rest and recuperation as much as any of the patients, I suppose.'

'I hope you find what you're seeking at Easterwood,' Ben said softly. 'I have.'

Jenny was about to ask him more about the house, anything to get off personal problems, then she tensed, aware that he was staring at someone beyond her, his expression inscrutable. She didn't need expensive radar equipment to know that Rachel Bonner had just entered the restaurant.

'Rachel's here, but I guess you know that,' he commented. 'Your defence shield was raised just then.'

'Oh! Is it that obvious? I'm sorry,' Jenny murmured, feeling nothing of the sort.

'It probably isn't obvious to other people, but sure as hell *I* notice it.' There was an edge to Ben's voice, and Jenny shot him a puzzled glance. Not that she had any reason to feel puzzled, she reflected after a moment. It was obvious how he felt about Rachel, and she would have to be careful to keep out of that lady's way.

A faint cloud of perfume hung in the air as Rachel approached their table, not even pretending surprise. 'I thought you would bring Jenny here!' she said lightly, while Ben rose, his face expressionless.

The waiter hastily brought up another chair, and a smiling and confident Rachel sat down. 'Thanks! I know you two want to talk shop, Jenny, but I hope you don't mind my joining you?'

Large tawny eyes were turned upon Jenny, who said quietly, 'Of course I don't mind. Why should I? But no, we weren't talking shop. I think that should be left to working hours, don't you?'

'Yes, I suppose so,' Rachel agreed. 'Only I thought that must be why Ben had invited you.' Despite the smile, which remained on her face, her eyes were cold. Unhappy eyes, Jenny thought, wishing she could make friends with the other woman. She knew only too well what it was like, being wrapped up in one's own misery, unable to communicate with others, tell them how she felt. Keep smiling and singing through all difficulties, that was the way. But it was unfair! The patients had someone to turn to, could unburden themselves to the nurses and doctors—why couldn't the staff do likewise?

'Busily replanning the clinic, Jenny?' Ben's calm

voice broke into her thoughts, but she merely shrugged.

'No, not exactly. It's just an idea I had. Forget it for now.' But she wouldn't forget the embryo of a scheme that was hatching in her brain. Time enough to tell him about it when she had given the matter more thought.

Rachel held the conversation together, and she and Ben chatted amiably throughout the remainder of the meal, Rachel choosing only a salad as her main course. Ben drew Jenny into the conversation at every opportunity, but most of the time she was content just to listen. The clinic was touched on briefly, but not patients, of course, and Jenny was surprised to learn that it was Ben Moran himself who had been born at Easterwood. That explained a good deal.

'Someone said a member of staff had known the place as home,' Jenny said during a brief pause in Rachel's chatter, 'but I didn't realise it was you. Does it bother you much, seeing your home turned into a hospital, losing its home-like character?' she wanted to know.

Before Ben could answer, Rachel put in, 'Of course it bothers him! How would you feel, knowing you had been pushed aside to——?'

Jenny intercepted the warning glance that went from psychiatrist to therapist, effectively stopping Rachel in mid-sentence.

'Sorry, Ben,' Rachel muttered, and Jenny almost said the same thing. She hadn't meant her remark to hurt Ben but she rather wished he had let Rachel finish what she was about say.

It was Ben himself who turned the conversation on to less contentious issues, telling Jenny about the outings that were planned for the patients during the summer. He leaned forward a little, his face only inches from Jenny's own, and this time it was Rachel who appeared to be out of the picture. 'We try to help patients lead as normal a life as possible while they're at the clinic, and we like staff to become involved,' he said.

'What sort of outings have you planned? I know they'll be taken shopping as a matter of routine but what about some of the stately homes or castles?' Jenny put in, his enthusiasm firing her own. 'Then there's the theatre. We could——'

'Our schedule of visits was planned months ago, Jenny,' Rachel said quickly. 'I don't think we can alter it now—do you, Ben?'

'I don't see why not. If Jenny has anywhere specific in mind, we could get the committee to consider it. Everything comes down to committees, Jenny,' Ben said lightly.

'If your schedule is already full, I wouldn't want to cause problems,' she said, her chin tilting a little, 'but if I find somewhere that isn't on the schedule, I'll certainly bring it before the committee. Which one, by the way?'

Ben chuckled huskily. 'Ah, that's a well-kept secret! We have so many, even I don't know about them all! Rachel's the one for sorting out who belongs to what. Aren't you, Rachel?' The smile he turned upon his colleague was warm, and to Jenny it seemed as if the sun had come out in the middle of the restaurant. How wonderful to have someone smile at *her* that way.

Lloyd. Yes, Lloyd. Funny how her thoughts always went winging back to him. Now his smiles were for her mother, and that hurt, far more than if he had run off with someone else. To have one's own *mother* snatch selfishly at her daughter's love, that hurt beyond measuring. Yet, was it selfish of Angie? Perhaps she, too, had fallen under a stronger spell. A spell rather like that cast by the Buccaneer, perhaps.

A feeling of coldness settled in the pit of Jenny's stomach. No, she *definitely* wasn't falling under any-

one's spell! Once bitten, twice shy, that was Sister
Jenny Fraser!

The Artful Pheasant boasted a dance-floor, small but
certainly large enough for about a dozen couples, and
Jenny saw Rachel glance wistfully at the couples as the
music began. It was an old-fashioned waltz, a love song
from some years previously that was enjoying a new
lease of life, and Jenny's eyes grew misty. It told of
unrequited love that wouldn't die, of a heart broken
into countless pieces. Of course, that sort of thing was
very commercial, and probably the composer had cried
all the way to the bank, but it affected her just the
same.

Ben had to speak twice to her before she really came
to, and it wasn't until Rachel laughed that Jenny
realised anyone was speaking. 'Sorry, I was miles
away,' she apologised briefly. 'Is it time to go?'

'Don't be silly, the evening's only just begun,' Rachel
said firmly, and Jenny shot her a perplexed glance.

'I thought you had to get back to the children? It's
getting on now, anyway, and I'm on duty tonight,'
Jenny reminded her.

Rachel's face brightened. 'I'd completely forgotten,'
she said, the look she gave Jenny giving a lie to her
words. 'I'll drive you back if you like, give Ben a rest.
He can relax here for a while.' Rachel gathered up her
bag and stole and was already on her feet before Jenny
could respond, the suddenness of Rachel's action
taking her by surprise.

She could hardly deny that Ben might need a rest,
but she felt that Rachel's driving left something to be
desired. A taxi might be a safer proposition and she
was about to tell them both firmly that *she* was going
home by taxi, when Ben solved the problem, though in
a way that obviously didn't suit Rachel Bonner. Or
Jenny, either, come to that, but for a different reason.

'It isn't *that* late, so there's time for me to give both

of you a whirl around the dance-floor,' Ben said pleasantly, a smile lurking around his mouth. 'And, since you're the newest member of staff, I'll dance with you first, Jenny.' He got up and waited, and an astonished Jenny found herself agreeing. His action left her little choice, but being whirled around the floor in the arms of the Buccaneer would be bitter-sweet.

Rachel's mouth tightened, but the smile she turned upon them both seemed genuine. Only Jenny saw the carefully reined-in anger. Oh, dear, she thought, another black mark for Sister Fraser! It was too bad of Ben. After all, she had to work with the woman. If Rachel felt she was a rival for the psychiatrist's affections, it would make collaborating in the care of patients extremely difficult.

The small band had turned to playing an even smoochier number by the time Jenny got to her feet, but if Ben noticed the reluctance with which she put her hand in his he gave no sign of it. Let him think she was still pining for Lloyd. That was her only defence. It was no lie, either.

'One of my favourite tunes,' he commented, as he held her closer than Jenny thought wise—or necessary. 'Don't tense up. Relax,' he commanded, but that was too much for Jenny, and she raised her face to his, her eyes sparking.

'I think I have every reason to be tense,' she said sharply, and was disconcerted to hear him chuckle.

'Have you? Now why is that, I wonder?' he said softly, his hand warm on her back. She had discarded her suit jacket, and was vibrantly aware of his body through the thin blouse. Earlier, she had thought the restaurant pleasantly cool, but not now!

She took refuge in anger. 'Rachel and I have to work together. I know I shan't see much of her on nights, but, even so, there's no point in making her jealous,' she said, a little unwisely.

'Are we making her jealous? There's nothing going on between Rachel and me, if that was the question.' Ben sounded amused, and Jenny flushed, realising she had given away more than she had intended.

'No, that wasn't the question! It's just that—oh, forget it. Thank you for the dinner, anyway. The food was superb,' she rushed on, anxious to change the subject.

'I'm glad. The sauce they served with the chicken is a speciality of the restaurant. We must come again,' he added, then disconcerted her by drawing her closer. She could feel his warm breath on her cheek, and she tensed even more, hating him at that moment. Yet. . . *We must come again.* Despite her good resolutions, Jenny had to admit that, if the 'we' was just Ben and herself, the idea was one she whole-heartedly agreed with!

Ben said nothing further, but she knew he must feel the fluttering of her poor heart, perhaps hear it beating. Then, when they returned to the table, an eager Rachel rushed into Ben's arms. This time the tune was up-tempo, and Jenny was glad. At least he couldn't be holding Rachel against his chest, smiling into her eyes, warming her with——

Abruptly Jenny cut off her thoughts. They were too dangerous. She contented herself, instead, by glancing around the restaurant. Their table was in an alcove by a huge bay window which overlooked the front drive. Outside, hundreds of fairy-lights had come on, and they shone out into the twilight. She had the absurd desire to stroll among them, hand in hand with Ben the Buccaneer.

Then the fact that it *was* twilight hit her, and she glanced at her watch. She ought to have been changed into her uniform about now! Ben must have known, surely? It really was too bad of him.

Glancing about for the couple, she couldn't at first

locate them, then she realised the band was playing a selection of tunes, not just the one, and Ben and Rachel must have stayed on the floor. Yet she looked in vain for Rachel's saffron-coloured dress, and had just decided to leave a note with the waiter before hurrying home, when she saw a tearful Rachel coming from the direction of the balcony. Behind her, face like thunder, was Ben.

Shock held Jenny motionless for a moment. They were having a lovers' tiff, there was no doubt about that. Then, quickly, she pulled herself together. What business was it of hers?

Yet Ben had assured her there was nothing between them, and it hurt more than she cared to admit that he had lied to her. Just like—— Just in time, she put the thought firmly out of her mind. What Ben said, or did, was no concern of hers. If he wanted an affair with Rachel, fine, wonderful, it didn't matter. But *she* wasn't going to be caught in the middle, not this time!

'I should be on duty about now.' With an effort, Jenny kept her voice even. 'I'll take a taxi and leave you to——'

Ben didn't let her finish the sentence. 'I brought you, I'll take you back. I have an article to write, anyhow. Let's go.'

Within a matter of minutes, a startled Jenny found herself in Ben's car, but he didn't join her straight away. 'I have to see Rachel off, then I'll be back,' he said curtly, then strode off to the other side of the car park where Rachel's sporty red car was just starting up.

Jenny watched them exchange a few words, then Rachel roared away, leaving Ben staring after her for a long moment, before he headed back towards his own car.

'I'm sorry. Things didn't work out as I planned,' he said, his voice as grim as his expression. 'Rachel——'

He hesitated, and impulsively Jenny put her hand on his arm.

'I understand, Ben. Do you think she should be driving? She seems overwrought. . .' Jenny's voice died away. Ben didn't need her to tell him that.

'She's frequently overwrought. I keep telling her to take some leave, but that won't help matters. She has to learn to cope. Let's get you on duty, shall we?' Ben turned to her, the upset with Rachel apparently forgotten.

Jenny nodded, averting her gaze. 'Yes, I mustn't be too late, it should prove an interesting night, with one patient in particular.'

'You mean Anne Bomford?' Ben's tone was noncommittal as they headed south towards her flat.

'Yes. She's going to test my patience, see how far she can go.' After an evening such as this, Jenny felt she wouldn't be able to cope if Anne played up, or there were any of the other emergencies that frequently occurred in a psychiatric hospital, but she didn't say so. Ben had enough problems. Yet. . . 'How did Sister Ross cope with Anne?' she asked, after a moment's thought. Her predecessor must have had *some* success at the clinic, surely?

'Shirley Ross,' Ben said flatly. 'She and Anne got on well, but——' He broke off, but Jenny couldn't afford to let it go like that. Everyone seemed reluctant to discuss the woman's abilities—or shortcomings.

'I need to know, Ben.' Jenny was nothing if not determined. 'There's some mystery about Sister Ross, and it's none of my business, but if *her* attitude is going to affect the way Anne and the others relate to *me*, then it becomes my business. On my first day, Fay Whalley said——' She stopped suddenly. 'She wasn't at my interview! Fay, I mean. I wonder why?'

'So many unanswered questions, Jenny. Forget it for now, will you? I'll tell you all about Shirley some day, *and* Fay. As for Anne, she needs a light hand on the reins, but once she's been reassessed I'm going to see that she doesn't return to the clinic. Will that do?' Ben turned the car off the dual carriageway, then swung hard left along a bumpy country lane.

'Yes, thank you, sir,' Jenny said meekly, and Ben laughed.

'Les was right—you *are* good for me,' he commented, concentrating on the narrow lane.

'I'm glad I'm good for somebody,' Jenny said wryly, then turned wondering eyes upon her companion as the car came to a halt. Ben eased himself round in the seat, sliding one arm along the back of Jenny's seat.

'Oh, Jenny, don't!' he said brokenly.

'Don't what?' She sat perfectly still, hardly daring to breathe. His eyes *were* black, she noticed in passing, not the dark brown she had at first thought. Then all coherent thought left her as his lips met hers. She felt him undo her seatbelt, then his arms enfolded hers, and she tried to melt into them, seeking sanctuary like some frightened little animal.

Ben half turned her so that her back was against his broad chest. His embrace didn't slacken, and she leant against him, eyes closed. She could feel the heat of his hands, which were clasped firmly across her abdomen, and, gently, she began to stroke the dark hairs on his wrists, wishing she had the right to remain here, in his arms. Think of Lloyd, she reminded herself silently, but could not.

Ben's lips brushed across her hair, his teeth began to nibble experimentally at her ear, and Jenny kicked off her shoes, wishing this moment could go on forever, wishing they need not return to the real world. Wishing she wasn't due on duty and could go home with Ben. . . No!

He released her abruptly, even before she began to struggle. Perhaps remembering I'm not Rachel, she

thought resentfully. Face flushed, she moved back into
her own seat, well aware that she'd been nearly sitting
on his lap. She had felt the stirrings of Ben's desire, a
desire to more than match her own. He might think
she was an easy lay. A pillow-friend—wasn't that what
they called them? And was *that* one of Shirley's
shortcomings?

Ben was appalled at what he had so nearly done. He
deserved to be struck off! Just when Jenny needed
TLC, he had wanted to offer something quite different.
'It's still Tuesday.' His voice was harsh, self-accusing.
'My wife's birthday.'

A shocked Jenny couldn't find words, as the car
accelerated away, leaving her only enough time to
settle into her seatbelt. His wife! Rachel? No, not
Rachel. Shirley Ross?

Bewildered and more hurt than she would have
believed possible, Jenny turned on him. No way was
she going to substitute for his wife!

'Should you be wining and dining another woman on
your wife's birthday? She must be wondering where
you've got to—or does she know you well enough to
guess?' she rushed on, wanting to hurt him as she had
been hurt. Of course, she had surmised he was married,
but nothing had been said of his wife at the clinic, and
she had foolishly let herself think he was free.

Ben didn't answer, and Jenny turned away from him.
No, he had no answer to her accusation, so it must be
true. Perhaps his wife had learned to live with his
womanising. Poor soul. She felt tears pricking the
backs of her eyes, and she bit her lip, drawing blood.
He mustn't see her weakness. Men were all alike! They
took all they——

She wasn't to finish her thought, for Ben made an
emergency stop, and she was propelled forward. The
seatbelt took the strain, but she was left gasping for
breath.

'Jenny? Are you all right?'

She nodded. Then she saw: they had reached a small crossroads, and Rachel's car was parked awkwardly across the top of the lane, half on the verge, half jutting out into the path of any traffic coming from Hastings.

'Rachel, *Rachel*!' Ben's voice was hoarse with emotion as he flung himself out of the car, leaving a dazed Jenny to follow, hoping against hope that nothing dreadful had happened to Rachel Bonner.

No matter what Ben might say, no matter that he had a wife, it was obvious that Rachel loved him—and he loved Rachel.

CHAPTER SEVEN

WHEN Jenny reached them, a seemingly unhurt Rachel was sitting on the grass verge, with Ben squatting beside her, one arm about her shoulders.

Rachel lit a cigarette, with hands that trembled slightly, then gazed at Jenny in surprise. 'Why is everyone rushing about?' she asked, drawing on the cigarette, then taking it out and glancing down at it before wrinkling her nose in distaste. 'I keep giving it up—or trying to, but. . .'

Gently Ben prised the cigarette from Rachel's grasp and extinguished it. 'Keep trying,' he said softly. 'You don't want anyone to think you're short on will-power, do you, honey?'

Rachel smiled at him, and Jenny half turned away, feeling that she was intruding. As long as Rachel wasn't hurt, that was all that mattered. She made her way back to the car, deciding it was best to leave them together, but she didn't get in. She needed fresh air and the chance to think.

The slight breeze had died down now, and the evening was calm and warm. A golden evening, Jenny reflected, an evening for strolling with a lover, murmuring sweet words, or talking in that inconsequential way that lovers had, speaking of nothing in particular, but touching on everything. Spring—this was the time for lovers, wasn't it? Her mind slid once more to her mother, who mustn't be called Mummy, but always Angie because it made her feel younger. An Angie who was only seventeen years older than Jenny herself. Perhaps it was hard being the mother of a teenage girl, hard because you looked younger than you were and didn't want to own to being *that* old. And, once Angie's pretty looks faded, would Lloyd still be interested? Would Angie have to fight time as well as other women in the effort to keep him?

For the first time since she had found them in each other's arms, Jenny understood how her mother felt. And, with understanding, came forgiveness. Of a sort, anyway. The wound might never heal properly, but already the pain was lessening.

In the background, she became aware that Rachel's voice was raised, but she couldn't hear Ben's reply. He would reason with her, show the calmness and patience that he had in abundance, coax her gently into facing whatever demon drove her so hard. We couldn't run away from our demons—they had to be faced sooner or later, and Jenny wondered whether she would have the courage to deal with her own.

She glanced about her, surprised to find that she had been walking along the lane, and thankful that this arm of the crossroads was little used. There was nothing to see here, just high banks on one side, fields on the other. Over in the distance rose the South Downs, and ahead of her the lane meandered along, with a stream running across and under it, going nowhere in particular as far as Jenny could tell.

Water was soothing, even so little as this, and she gazed down at the celandine-covered bank for a moment, watching the stream as it moved a fraction then caught on the weeds which threatened to choke it, then moved along a bit more. For a moment, Rachel and Ben were—— No, not Ben. Ben could never be forgotten. Jenny was vibrantly aware of Ben the Buccaneer, no matter how much she might deny it to herself.

But the attraction would have to be denied, she told herself firmly. She had fancied herself immune, but now realised she wasn't. Love didn't come into it, of course. No, it was a spell he had cast over her, a momentary sexual attraction. Nothing more than that.

Work, work and more work, that was the answer. And, if her schemes for an occupational health nurse for the Easterwood came to fruition, she would have more than enough to do. She could——

Jenny tensed, then slowly turned around. Ben was only a few feet away, watching her. He stood relaxed, hands in trouser pockets, that little smile on his mouth. She couldn't have heard him, and he hadn't spoken, yet she had known he was there, would always know he was there.

'Sorry. Do you want to get back now?' she said, her voice a trifle strained. He would pick that up for sure. 'I didn't realise I'd come so far.'

'No, we never do,' Ben agreed huskily. 'Rachel's coming with us. I'll move her car somewhere safer and call back for it later. I can't have her drive in that state.'

He sounded oddly defensive, and Jenny smiled. 'No, of course you can't. No one would expect you to. Or how about me driving your car, and you driving Rachel's? That way I might get on duty no more than an hour late!' She tried to make a joke of it, but it fell flat. Tears weren't very far away, and she turned slightly, not wanting him to see her face until she was in control of herself again.

'Jenny. . .' Her name was softly spoken, more of a caress than a word, but she didn't want his pity, his understanding, particularly after that passionate embrace they had shared. She just wanted to be left in peace to lick her wounds.

Suddenly she became angry. What right had Ben to offer her comfort? 'Don't touch me!' she said, as he moved nearer. 'I'm all right, really. See to Rachel— I'll be along in a minute,' she went on, more quietly, feeling a fool. Ben hadn't been about to touch her; it was all in her mind. A fine mental nurse *she* was!

Ben's hands gripped hers. 'Jenny, look at me,' he commanded, and a fierce pride made her obey.

Forcing a smile to her lips, she gazed into the dark depths of his eyes. 'Sorry! I'm over-tired. I haven't got used to nights again yet. And with finding Rachel like that. . .' She let the sentence trail off, hoping he would accept it as an excuse. The heat from his hands was spreading to her own, heating her whole body, and she wished he would let go, wishing at the same time that he would not.

'Jenny.' He said her name again, and never had it sounded lovelier. It was a perfectly ordinary name, but on his lips it was the most beautiful name in the world.

Jenny's lips parted, and she swayed towards him. Then she remembered Rachel. And Ben's wife.

Abruptly she turned away from him and began to walk back towards the cars. Forget Ben, she told herself. Concentrate on work. That embrace in the car had been a momentary weakness on his part—and on hers.

Her sensible summing-up of the episode didn't stop her from taking a detour via Southdown Road, once she was changed and on her way to the clinic. Southdown Road was quiet and tree-lined, with perhaps six or seven detached houses, set well back, and she couldn't decide which was his. Only one house showed a light. By now, it was nearly dark, and she chided herself for going out of her way. Wasn't she supposed to forget Ben?

Ben had told the clinic staff of Rachel's accident, and the day nurses had gone by the time Jenny finally arrived on duty. 'Are there any problems?' she asked the staff nurse, Beryl Templar, who pulled a face.

'It depends what you mean by problems. There isn't anything, really, but Anne Bomford's in a funny mood—funny peculiar,' Beryl added. 'She's restless and keeps muttering to herself, though she's perfectly pleasant, even helpful. When she found you hadn't arrived, she offered to help with the evening medicine round, so I let her. She poured out the juice for me and handed it to the patients while we——' the nurse indicated the student '—gave out the medication. So she was a help, I have to admit that, but. . .'

Jenny understood. An experienced nurse soon got a 'feel' for the patients and could sometimes stop trouble before it had time to begin, just by knowing the patients or a particular patient so well that she recognised even the slightest change in that person's expression or demeanour. She herself would be at a disadvantage for some time to come, until she really got to know the patients. With those who were regulars, like Sophie Clary, she could bone up on the background, read through their case-notes, and perhaps find a pattern to the patient's behaviour, but with others it would be more difficult—a case of playing it by ear.

Anne Bomford, naturally, had a thick case folder, since she was one of those who came in regularly, but Jenny had dipped into the case-notes and couldn't see any pattern, or at least one she could recognise. Women like that were a danger, and Anne would repay careful watching. Although Ben had told her they didn't accept psychopaths, there was no doubt that Anne had psychopathic tendencies. She suffered periodic bouts of depression, which was why she was a patient there.

Beryl gave her a run-down of the patients, including Mrs Lawrence, who, once again, was talking of discharging herself. Then Jenny issued instructions to the staff before going in search of Stella Lawrence. Anne was the bigger problem, but was best left to those who knew her.

Mrs Lawrence wasn't hard to find, since she was wandering restlessly about the rooms and along the thickly carpeted corridor. 'Sorry I'm late,' Jenny said, with a warm smile. 'How are you, Mrs Lawrence? I hear your husband visited this afternoon.'

'Oh, yes, he did,' the patient said, without much enthusiasm. 'He couldn't stay long, poor darling. There's an important meeting coming up and——' She hesitated, giving Jenny a sharp look. 'There's talk of getting rid of him. Making him give up his chairmanship,' she went on, as Jenny gazed at her perplexedly.

'I see,' she said slowly. This must have some bearing on Mrs Lawrence's condition. 'Is it anything you want to talk about? I'm just off to do a quick round, but you could pop into the office later, if you would like to?' she offered. Mrs Lawrence shrugged, then pulled her expensive silk dressing-gown more tightly around her, as if to repel boarders. It was a defensive gesture, like folding one's arms.

She opened her mouth as if to say more, then closed it again, before walking rapidly away from Jenny. Then Anne Bomford hove into view, singing quietly to herself. Trailing along behind her was Sophie Clary, and Jenny's heart sank. *Two* problems together—two minds dreaming up mischief!

Anne greeted her cheerfully enough. 'You're very late, Sister. We thought you weren't coming. Didn't we, Sophie?'

Sophie merely nodded, then smiled dreamily at Jenny, without really seeing her, perhaps. 'I thought I wasn't coming, as well,' Jenny said, wondering whether she should stay with the two young women, try to work out what *might* happen, then decided against it. She would finish her round, then concentrate on Mrs Lawrence.

Stella Lawrence seemed glad to join her in the quiet room later on, but she refused to sit, preferring to pace

restlessly up and down the quite large room. It had
once been a sitting-room, and was still furnished as
such, without the ubiquitous television, and with the
addition of a writing table and chair. Comfortable
chairs abounded, and there was a settee over by the
window, where Jenny seated herself and slipped off
her duty shoes. It occurred to her that in such an
informal setting it would be more appropriate if she
wore her own clothes. Another matter she had to
discuss with Ben the Buccaneer!

'You're smiling, Sister. Is there something funny
about a middle-aged woman being incarcerated in this
place?' Mrs Lawrence's voice was sharp.

'It was just a passing thought. I was thinking how
out of place I feel here!' Jenny waved a hand to indicate
the genteel room. 'This was a home once, someone's
sitting-room, where tea and dainty little sandwiches
were dispensed, the latest gossip exchanged. Oh, I
don't know, it wasn't meant to be part of a clinic,' she
went on slowly, and the patient nodded.

'I know what you mean. I feel that, too. Someone
said it used to be Dr Ben's home. Did you know that?
Apparently he spent his childhood here, then someone
died. His parents, I suppose. The house passed to
another branch of the family. Some cousin, or so the
domestic was telling me, and poor Dr Ben was home-
less.' Mrs Lawrence paused, then sat down beside
Jenny, her ankles neatly crossed. 'I don't quite know
where Australia came in. Was he adopted, do you
know?'

Feeling that she shouldn't be discussing Ben with a
patient, Jenny shook her head. 'I've no idea. Dr Ben is
my boss, though, and I don't think he would like
it if——'

'No, no, of course he wouldn't,' Mrs Lawrence broke
in. 'I forgot. Anyway, he might be around tonight,

mightn't he? Then I can ask him myself.' She smiled a trifle wistfully.

'He might be in, but I doubt it. I saw him earlier and he had one or two problems to sort out,' Jenny said carefully, not wanting to mention Rachel Bonner's near-accident. 'I saw Rachel as well. She's your therapist, isn't she? How is the treatment going?'

'Treatment!' Mrs Lawrence almost spat the word at her. 'I hardly think it's treatment, Sister. Trying to prevent me carrying out my rituals isn't much of a therapy. I came here to be cured!'

'That's what Rachel's trying to do, my dear. But you have to meet her halfway. You can't be helped if you don't want to be. I know your rituals are comforting,' Jenny went on, 'and perhaps you think they're necessary to your well-being, but that isn't so.'

'Well, of course they aren't. And yes, I *do* want to be rid of this endless hand-washing, rearranging things, then rearranging them again, but. . .'

'What sort of programme has Rachel arranged for you?' Jenny asked, after a few moments.

'Oh, we have a contract. Would you believe that? It sounds like a business transaction, doesn't it?' Mrs Lawrence sat up. 'Something my husband might arrange!'

'It's one of the "in" things in psychiatry. You and Rachel agreed the terms between you, didn't you?'

'Mm, yes. At least I had some say in the matter. I agreed certain clauses, or rather I agreed not to do certain things, such as washing my hands so often, or re-making my bed after the domestic has already made it. But it's never right, Sister! I have to be sure everything is aired, so I strip it again, then make it up.'

'Then strip it once more?' Jenny suggested, beginning to see a pattern to the patient's behaviour.

'Yes, several times. I don't count things, though. That woman in the next bed, Miss Millington—Ivy.

She counts things: the pattern on the wallpaper, the flowers on the bedspread, the number of tiles in the bathroom. She's getting better now, though. She told me she believed something dreadful would happen if she missed counting, and if she was interrupted while she was counting she had to begin again. How awful! At least I'm not that bad.'

'There's always someone worse,' Jenny agreed. 'How does your husband view your being here?'

There was what might have been termed a 'pregnant pause', which Jenny felt was significant, then Mrs Lawrence attempted a laugh, which didn't come off. 'He thinks I'm being silly. He hated coming here this afternoon,' she confided. 'He says it's an excuse to get away from home—from him.'

'And is it?' Jenny asked quietly, but there was no reply. Mrs Lawrence started her agitated pacing up and down again, so Jenny got up, reaching for her shoes.

'I'd better be going, I think. I was terribly late and I promised to do some teaching. We have a general student,' she went on, realising that the patient wanted to change the subject, 'and this is a learning situation for her. I try to explain that mental nursing is just as much a skill as surgical or medical nursing.'

'Yes, I realise that. You've been very kind, Sister. Everyone has, but I don't believe I shall stay,' Stella Lawrence said quietly, not meeting Jenny's gaze.

'That's your decision, of course, but don't make firm plans to leave before talking to Dr Ben, will you?' Jenny urged. 'He'll be on the ward tomorrow—there's a round at eleven. See him then, if you can.'

The woman nodded, then sat, head bowed, as Jenny left the room. It was going to be one of those nights, she could feel it in her bones.

Ben didn't put in an appearance that night, and Jenny wasn't sure whether to be glad or sorry. Of course, he was probably busily soothing Rachel, though the therapist had seemed her old self by the time Jenny had left them. The three of them had piled into the old car Ben was driving, and Jenny had been dropped off at her flat first, while he presumably took Rachel home.

Perhaps he had remained the night there. The children would need seeing to, and Ben was a caring man. It wasn't likely he would have left Rachel to cope alone with her children.

A caring man. How wonderful that sounded—in theory. Yet he appeared not to care for his wife, and that was something Jenny found difficult to understand. '*My wife's birthday*.' Ben's words echoed and re-echoed in her head.

Sighing a little, she settled down to write the report. 'Three o'clock and all's well,' she felt like writing, but that might tempt fate! Apart from the fact that Anne Bomford remained restive, there wasn't anything in particular to report so far.

Unfortunately, if one patient was restless it often communicated itself to the others. Mrs Lawrence was still awake, and as she passed the bedroom earlier Jenny had heard the murmur of voices. Presumably that was Mrs Lawrence and Miss Millington, who had struck up a friendship. Then there was Sophie, who had been flitting about until gone midnight, despite medication. She——

The faint sound, the feeling of an unknown presence, that had disturbed her the previous night, came again, but this time Jenny was quicker. If one of the patients was given to nocturnal wandering, or there was a prowler about, Sister Fraser intended to settle the matter once and for all!

CHAPTER EIGHT

JENNY rushed from the office, shining her powerful torch along the corridor, and was just in time to see the fire door close. Knowing she ought to ring for assistance, but anxious that the intruder shouldn't get away, she switched on the lights in the corridor, then set off in pursuit.

Ben went that way sometimes, through the room which was used only for private meetings, then out into the ballroom. It wasn't him tonight, though, and if it was a patient she might manage to lure her—or him—back again.

Cautiously Jenny pushed against the heavy door, then shone her torch into the room. It was huge, with heavy, cumbersome furniture, and rather creepy. She reached for the light-switch, but the chandelier, set high in the ceiling, illuminated only that section of the room, leaving the rest of it in shadow. She decided that discretion was the better part of valour—there was no point in being too adventurous!

She was about to return to the office to ring Fay Whalley, who was the duty nursing officer, when she thought she heard a muffled sound. She would be all kinds of a fool if she investigated on her own—yet it could be a patient in distress. There was really no choice. If she went back to the office, whoever was in the room might do something rash.

'Sophie?' she called softly, wondering if it *was* her. 'Is that you? It's Sister Jenny. I'm just going to have a cup of cocoa. Would you like one?'

She listened, but the sound wasn't repeated, and she

had no idea from which part of the room it had come, or even if she had imagined it.

'Sophie? Sophie, it's Sister Fraser—Jenny.' Jenny waited, hardly daring to breathe, but there was no response, at least from that direction. But her staff nurse's voice reached her, breaking the spell.

'Jenny? Are you all right? I was just coming to find you.' Beryl Templar joined her in the doorway of the shadowy room. 'Anne's disappeared again.'

Jenny sighed. 'Anne?' she called into the room. 'If you're there, show yourself, please.' Her tone of voice reflected how she felt. Whereas she believed Sophie Clary genuinely needed help, she hadn't a lot of time for Anne. It was an unfortunate distinction to make and Jenny knew it. They all needed help, the socio-paths of this world just as much as the schizophrenics, the depressed, the plain anxious, but there was some-thing cold and calculating in Anne's manner towards everyone, and Jenny couldn't help thinking the girl might have chosen this night to best the new night sister. Well, she wouldn't be bested!

'Come on, who *is* there?' she asked sharply, then a figure appeared from behind a dust-sheeted settee. Beryl cried out in alarm, and the person hesitated.

Not wanting to lose the initiative, Jenny advanced into the room. Then the wandering beam of her torch found the thick-set figure of Simon Jenkins. 'Simon!' He was the last person Jenny had expected to find, and quickly she swung the beam away from his face as he came hesitantly towards her. 'Simon—are you all right?'

He seemed dazed, and twice he nearly stumbled. 'Yes, I'm fine, Sister. I . . . I must have fallen asleep,' he muttered.

'Bed's the place for sleep,' Jenny said calmly, relieved yet still wondering. Surely the prosaic Simon Jenkins wasn't meeting Anne on the quiet? He couldn't have fallen asleep, for she had seen the door close only minutes before.

'Come and have some cocoa,' she urged, linking her arm in his. 'I thought you were Sophie at first—or Anne Bomford,' she added, then felt him shudder.

'Don't mention that creature to me! She keeps following me! At least. . . No, perhaps she doesn't,' Simon conceded, his smile wry as they sat down in the warm office. 'She just wanders around a lot. It gives me the creeps!'

You and me both, Jenny thought. 'She's gone off somewhere. Did you see her at all? Oh, hello!'

'Good evening,' a voice said coldly, and Fay Whalley walked into the office. 'Staff Nurse said you needed assistance, but I see you're coping.'

Was there an accusation in the nursing manager's voice? Jenny rather felt there was, and Simon certainly did, for he rose hurriedly, his long, rather doleful face red with embarrassment. His dressing-gown barely covered him, and he was wearing only pyjama trousers.

'I'll get back to bed, then, Sister,' he said quickly, but Jenny shook her head. She wanted to find out what was troubling him, and Fay had no right to offer criticism, even if it was unspoken!

'It's all right, Simon. Go to the kitchen, and one of the nurses will make you some cocoa. I'll be along in a while. I still have to find Anne Bomford.'

Fay Whalley grimaced after Simon left. 'Anne's always missing, but she'll turn up.' She sank down opposite Jenny, a thin smile on her face. 'I don't wish to be critical, Jenny, but it's best not to be alone with a male patient. Ben never goes unchaperoned, and I feel you should be as careful as he is. Psychiatric nurses are vulnerable—you don't need me to tell you that.'

'Like Shirley Ross, for instance?' Jenny probed, and the manager nodded.

'Perhaps. You're very pretty. And young,' Fay went

on, making it sound less than a compliment. 'Be careful—that's all I'm saying. Now——' She got up, all briskness again. 'Shall we search for Anne?'

Apart from Anne, there was another patient missing. That, surprisingly, was Stella Lawrence. Miss Millington was sound asleep in the next bed, and Jenny didn't want to waken her, but had to do so when a search of the sitting-rooms failed to produce Mrs Lawrence. The other two patients in the room knew nothing about her.

'The last thing I remember, Sister, was Stella and Ivy whispering away, then I must have dropped off,' one woman said.

Ivy Millington looked startled, then uncomfortable, when Jenny woke her. 'Isn't Stella here, Sister? Surely it isn't time to get up yet? I've hardly been asleep an hour,' she complained.

Jenny smiled. 'I'm sorry. I hate being wakened before I'm ready to get up too, but we must find Mrs Lawrence. She isn't in the quiet-room, and we're just doing a spot check. So many of our people are restless tonight, and we have to count heads, I'm afraid. Where is Mrs Lawrence?'

'I don't know, to tell you the truth. She spoke about discharging herself, but I thought she was going to see Dr Ben tomorrow. Oh, no, that's today now,' Miss Millington went on drowsily. 'Her husband rang up and that upset her, but——'

'But he visited! She told me.' Perhaps she was trying to tell me more and I didn't listen properly, Jenny reflected sadly.

'Yes, I know, but he rang later. After you came on,' the patient continued. 'I don't know what it was all about.'

Jenny rather thought Ivy Millington knew more than she was saying, but no good would come of probing too deeply. 'You will tell me if you remember anything else, Miss Millington? I'm responsible for her, and I could lose my job if she has wandered off and dies in a ditch somewhere.'

Leaving the patient with that sombre warning, Jenny was about to lend a hand with the now full-scale search, when Lesley Bell came rushing up.

'It's all right, Sister! She's downstairs, with the old people!' When Jenny just stared, the aide went on, 'You know, the geriatric ward. We have a few elderly patients downstairs and——'

'You mean Anne?' Surely Mrs Lawrence wasn't there?

Lesley nodded. 'Yes, of course. I thought you were looking for her?'

'It's Mrs Lawrence I'm concerned about—she's disappeared now,' Jenny said briskly. 'Tell Beryl I'll be downstairs. I have to talk to Anne.'

'Stella? No, Sister, *I* haven't seen her.' Anne's face was a picture of innocence when at length Jenny found her. She was playing snakes and ladders with a nurse in the dayroom of the small geriatric ward. 'I haven't been outside tonight!' she added with a grin, and Jenny smiled, despite her worries.

The staff nurse in charge of the ward seemed surprised when Jenny asked why no one in the acute wing knew Anne was down there. 'She told me you wouldn't mind,' the nurse admitted. 'I suppose I should have checked, but Shirley Ross never bothered. Sorry, anyway.'

Because Sister Ross didn't care, Sister Fraser was supposed not to care, either. Well, she did! But Jenny accepted the apology calmly, and, after pointing out that she needed to know if any of her patients came down again, she hurried back upstairs.

She was justifiably annoyed about Anne, but her real worry was Stella Lawrence, and she felt that the fault was hers. Mrs Lawrence might have been silently asking for help, and, not receiving any, had perhaps decided to leave. Yet, unless someone let her out, she must still be in the building somewhere.

Although the outside doors were locked at night, this was to keep intruders out rather than patients in. Since all their patients were informal, any of them could, in theory, request the night porters to let them into the grounds.

In the case of Anne Bomford, this was a regular occurrence and apparently caused no comment, though Jenny expressed dismay when she belatedly found out. Resi had explained that it was part and parcel of the unstructured Easterwood routine. As long as the ward was notified that Anne was out, it did not pose a problem. On Monday night, Anne hadn't asked the porter. She had gone instead to the geriatric ward and been let out of the side-door.

It seemed rather a casual attitude to Jenny, though, to be fair, only Anne was accorded such a privilege. Sophie would never have been allowed out after dark, nor people with hypermanic ideas, nor anyone suicidal.

If any of the others wanted an evening stroll, a senior nurse had to give permission, and Jenny fully agreed with this sensible policy. An anxious patient or one suffering obsessional thoughts might well feel calmer after a solitary walk, or any of the night nurses would be only too happy to accompany them. Then, too, for patients to feel they were under lock and key, no longer in control of their own destinies, might well prove intolerable, and could seriously impede their eventual recovery. As Ben had said, the hospital must do the patient no harm!

Yet memory kept coming back of the patient who had gone missing at her previous hospital. She, too, hadn't been suicidal, and Jenny would have staked a year's salary on her being found alive and well, as full of herself as always. But she had died. Now there was

Stella Lawrence, obsessed with her rituals and resentful that the therapist was trying to take them away. Not suicidal, and yet. . .

An apologetic cough broke into Jenny's anguished thoughts as she prepared for the hand-over later. It was daylight now, the unending night really was over, and she felt drained of all strength. Yet she managed a wan smile for Simon Jenkins, who stood uncertainly by the door.

'Sorry I couldn't get back to you,' she apologised. 'It's been one of those nights! You were asleep when I checked, though.'

'I'm depressed—don't depressed people sleep a lot?' Simon remained where he was, perhaps recalling the nursing manager's attitude, but Jenny invited him in.

'Leave the door open, then no one can complain. I'm feeling depressed, too. There's still no sign of Mrs Lawrence,' Jenny went on, as Simon sat down. She let out a small sigh. Life was becoming more difficult, and she hadn't completed a week yet!

'Sorry—are we all a trial to you?' Simon asked wryly, but Jenny shook her head.

'No, it's just that I'm tired. After a week or two, I'll get into the swing of things again. Now, is there anything I can help you with?'

'I don't suppose so, really. I get down-hearted when I think about the future,' Simon admitted, staring at his hands. 'Rachel's helpful, but she reminds me of my wife! Firm and well in control of everything, loud voice, commanding manner. Thinking everyone else is . . .not really stupid, just incapable. Talking down to me. . .'

Jenny realised he was projecting his wife's traits on to Rachel. Whatever the therapist's faults, she was too good a nurse to talk down to a patient. 'Rachel isn't like that. She's softly spoken,' she put in.

'Yes. Did I say she wasn't? I'm sorry.' Simon buried

his face in his hands, but Jenny resisted the urge to put a comforting arm around him. It wouldn't do. A longing for Ben overcame her, and she set her mind to conjuring him up. He would know what to do for Simon.

But it didn't work. No Ben the Buccaneer materialised and she was left with a patient who would be better discussing his problems with another man, particularly if the problems were sexual ones. Well, he would just have to talk to the male staff nurse, Albert, who would be on duty shortly.

'I'm depressed, Sister,' Simon mumbled. 'It isn't just the. . .compulsions? Is that what you call them? Rachel has some fancy name for them but I can't remember.'

'Obsessive-compulsive neurosis,' Jenny said carefully.

'That means I'm neurotic, I suppose? I could stop checking things any time I wanted. It's all put on—all in my mind! Is *that* it?'

He was working himself into a fine lather and almost shouting, but Jenny felt it was best to let him pour out his anger, his resentment. What he really wanted was to tell his wife what he thought of her, but she doubted he would ever do that. Rachel must be put in the picture, but would she come in today?

'I'll tell Rachel how you feel,' Jenny assured him. 'She certainly doesn't think you incapable *or* neurotic. It's simply a term to distinguish your type of disorder from the more severe illnesses like schizophrenia or mania—people who hear voices or lose contact with reality. They're psychotic. These are just words,' she went on slowly, doubting if he fully understood. 'Dr Ben says we mustn't label patients, so you haven't been labelled "Simon Jenkins—Neurotic"!'

Simon broke into a smile, then met her eyes for the first time. 'I've been wallowing in self-pity, haven't I?'

He rose. 'I'd better let you get on, Sister—or may I call you Jenny?'

'Of course you may.' Jenny's smile lit up her pale, tired face.

'See you, then, Jenny!' Simon turned quickly and almost bumped into Ben Moran, whose assessing gaze enveloped them both.

After the patient left, Ben hovered in the doorway, his eyes cool. 'Is everything all right now, Jenny? About Stella Lawrence. I——'

'If you're blaming me for that, you can't blame me more than I do myself!' Jenny said sharply. 'I was in charge, and the fault is mine. Here.' She pushed the incident report sheet across to him. 'I've filled it in as far as I'm able. The entire house was searched in the night and as much of the grounds as we could. They've been——'

'Stella's turned up. Safe and well,' Ben added quickly, as Jenny's eyes grew wide with apprehension.

'She's safe? Oh, thank heaven!' Then her relief turned to anger. 'Why didn't someone tell me? I've been worrying myself sick here!' She still blamed herself for not checking on the woman earlier. 'Counting heads' was almost an automatic reflex in a psychiatric hospital, yet she hadn't.

'It's OK, Jenny—relax,' Ben ordered, putting out a hand towards her, then quickly withdrawing it as she flinched away. His voice was expressionless as he went on, 'Stella's husband picked her up just outside. Around three o'clock, as near as I can make out.'

'About the time I was writing the report and thinking "All's well",' said Jenny bitterly.

'She's safe—that's all that matters. I've just come from there.' Ben glanced at the chair Simon had vacated, then thought better of it. He was dead-beat but didn't want to relax with Jenny. She had the gift of making him feel comfortable and at ease. Then she would suddenly turn on him, eyes sparking as she contested some decision he'd made, and he found her far from comfortable—but highly desirable.

'Stella began planning it when he visited, and Mr Lawrence had to fit in with her plans. He's being booted out of his job and I guess he doesn't know *what* he's doing,' Ben went on reflectively.

'But why couldn't he let us know she was safe? We've had people out all night! Fay phoned to tell him his wife was missing, but he didn't say she was there.'

'He told Fay he didn't know where Stella was, but that we weren't to contact the police. He said he felt sure she would turn up! Fay thought Stella was at home when she rang—that's why she didn't trouble too much about it.'

Jenny reflected that it was a great pity Fay Whalley hadn't shared her thoughts, but refrained from comment.

'Stella was afraid we would come after her, I guess,' Ben went on grimly, 'and I did. I apologise for not getting here before—it's been some night!'

'No, Ben. It's all right—I'm sorry I hit the roof.' Jenny intended to have a few straightforward words with Fay but Ben wasn't to blame. He had done his best. Then she remembered. 'How's Rachel this morning?'

'Alive and well. That's about all I can say. I fixed breakfast for the kids and left them to it.'

So, Ben had spent the night there. 'You must be tired,' Jenny said quickly. 'I'll get Lesley to make you some coffee. And do you want breakfast?'

A slow smile touched the corners of his mouth. 'They've already got my coffee and rolls on the way, but thank you, Jenny.'

She smiled back, before remembering that she must not. 'What's going to happen about Stella now? Will she come as a day patient? She still needs treatment.'

'No, I won't have her on a day basis,' Ben said firmly. 'I've told them if the compulsions get worse— and they probably will—Mrs Lawrence will have to get in touch with the ward and we'll have her back, if there's a vacancy. *Next* time she has to obey a few rules.'

'I doubt if she will want to return,' Jenny said thoughtfully. 'She hated sharing a room at first. Couldn't some of the ladies have single rooms? I keep meaning to ask you.'

He considered for a moment. 'I feel inclined to say not. So many of them lead solitary lives, even in the midst of their families. They've no one to really talk to. They're told to pull themselves together or stop making a fuss, or labelled "Attention-seeking". Yes?' Ben raised a brow enquiringly, and Jenny nodded, his words giving her food for thought.

'That's why I like them to have company here. In single bedrooms they have more opportunity to brood. But we'll have a meeting about it, see what the day staff think,' Ben went on. 'Then we can talk out all our problems, can't we?'

His eyes seemed to bore deep into her soul, and Jenny wondered how many of *her* problems he could solve! 'That will be helpful,' she agreed. 'Anne Bomford is another problem, though. *Someone* must have let Mrs Lawrence out. Anne goes wandering at night,' she reminded him, 'though last night she insisted she hadn't been outside.'

'Shirley Ross used to let Anne out—until I heard about it,' Ben said tightly. 'And Resi still does. On Monday night a nurse from the old folks' ward unlocked the door for her, as you know. That's something that won't happen again, unless they ask your permission first. Anne helps make the beds down there, and the old people love her. She has a good relationship with the nurses, too, and I suppose they thought there was no harm in letting her out.'

'And they knew Sister Ross never minded,' Jenny said quietly. 'But someone told me it was in order for even the night porter to let Anne into the grounds if she wanted to stroll about in the dark!' She didn't intend bringing Resi's name into it, although she was sure her likeable colleague hadn't deliberately misled her.

Ben shook his head, then tried to slick his hair back. But that wayward lock defeated him, and he frowned, watched with interest by Jenny. 'That was Resi, I would guess—wishful thinking on her part! She and I have an ongoing battle over how much freedom to allow patients. She's had over twenty years' nursing experience and I value her judgement—so we compromise. Anne. . .' He paused, then gave in to his fatigue, settling his long body in the chair opposite Jenny's desk and surveying her from under half-closed lashes.

'Resi's allowed to let Anne out when she's in charge, even in the early hours of the morning, but if Anne wants to go out on one of your nights, then it's up to you. That's it in theory. In practice, it's a little different. On her previous admissions, the nurses have allowed Anne to wander at will, and old habits die hard. It might be unwise to change the rules now,' he said slowly, thinking that if he was to forbid Anne to go out at night the girl would take her resentment out on the new night sister. His poor Jenny wouldn't stand a chance.

No, she wasn't his! He was being a fool. Jenny's heart still belonged to that smarmy guy with the fancy tie and hand-made shoes. The fact that he was her stepfather couldn't alter that. Ben smiled grimly to himself. Suddenly he felt every one of his forty-one years. Jenny deserved better. There was nothing he could offer her. Not after Louise.

Jenny watched Ben wrestle with some inner turmoil. No doubt he was thinking of Rachel. Well, that was only natural, wasn't it?

'Resi believes Anne should be allowed out whenever she wishes, that to coop her up when she gets wanderlust is bad for her. Bad for everybody,' Ben's weary voice continued.

'Annoyance and pique turning to aggression, then perhaps to violence. Yes, I can see her point—particularly at night,' Jenny agreed. 'But I can't accept that there's one rule for a patient with aggressive tendencies and another for the rest. You're just rewarding the aggression.'

'We *all* have aggressive tendencies. Didn't I hear Simon yelling at you while I was at the other end of the corridor?'

'That's different!' Jenny said quickly, aware that Ben was right, to some extent. 'He needed to express his feelings, to get rid of his anger and——'

'Frustration,' Ben finished for her. 'It was acceptable behaviour from Simon. Yet if Anne started screaming at the nurses, you would label her "Aggressive tendencies, possibly violent if provoked". Is that right?'

'Yes, Dr Ben,' Jenny said meekly, but with a gleam in her eye.

'I'm glad you're becoming servile, Sister Jenny. You had me worried for a while!'

They laughed together, the laughter warming her. So did the knowledge that Ben was prepared to listen to her point of view, listen to Resi Astley's as well. That she and her nursing colleague held opposite views on some things didn't matter—the chief was prepared to give them both a fair hearing. He was a just man, and, if he and the behavioural therapist *were* having an affair, it made no difference to his abilities as a psychiatrist, nor as a boss. Jenny resolved to fight down

her unreasoning jealousy of Rachel, and work for a
harmonious relationship with them all.

The harmonious relationship with Rachel Bonner
didn't last long, though Jenny tried her best. As before,
they disagreed over Simon Jenkins, Rachel considering
he spent too much time talking over his problems at
night, leaving him tired and irritable during the day
when she wanted to work with him.

This was Thursday night, the last night on duty for
Jenny, and she and Rachel faced each other in the
interview-room. Rachel was coldly angry, seemingly
unable to accept that the new night sister might have a
part to play in Simon's treatment.

'Nights are for sleeping. *I* need an alert patient in
the mornings—not one who dozes off in a chair when
I'm talking to him!' The tawny eyes looked through
Jenny, who was irresistibly reminded of Sophie Clary.

'I take your point,' Jenny said calmly. 'And I do try
to discourage him but he needs to talk at night and
I'm——'

'Blonde and rather pretty,' Rachel broke in, to
Jenny's astonishment. 'Just like Shirley Ross! She used
to butt in, feeding the patients all sort of different
ideas. We have a plan for every patient, Jenny, and
Ben expects us to stick to it. The only changes come
from the patient himself. No one else,' Rachel insisted.

'I think it would be wrong to turn Simon away when
he wants to talk, but I wouldn't dream of trying to
change your patient-plan. But are you speaking to
me—or to Shirley Ross?' Jenny went on. 'It doesn't
necessarily follow that I hold the same views as Sister
Ross.' She waited, wondering if she had discovered the
real reason for Rachel's antagonism.

'No, it doesn't. I'm sorry,' Rachel said unexpectedly.
'I've been feeling a bit fraught lately. The children. . .'
The sentence trailed off, but Jenny didn't try to offer

words of comfort, feeling that Rachel would reject them. Now wasn't the time.

'Couldn't you ask for a few days off?' she suggested instead, but Rachel shook her head.

'We've so much work in, I daren't take time off. We're having another therapist, but she doesn't start till June, and Nina is only part-time.' Rachel paused, then shrugged. 'Anyway, I must go, and wish you a quiet night!'

'Last night was quiet—I can't expect two!' Jenny said lightly. 'I'll see you again next Monday, perhaps.'

'Perhaps,' Rachel agreed wanly, then glided away, pausing to speak to someone just outside the room. Then her distinctive laugh rang out, and Jenny's antennae warned her that Ben Moran was about.

Drat the man! Didn't he spend *any* part of the night at home? Of course, she acknowledged, but only to herself, she was pleased to know he was around. Once she was settled into her post, he would probably not appear so much. The first week in a senior position was always difficult, and she appreciated his helpful remarks about the patients, but. . .

But I wish you would leave me in peace, Ben the Buccaneer, she said silently, as she headed for the night sister's office. You're disturbing me more than you will ever know.

CHAPTER NINE

'SOPHIE? It's Sister Jenny.' Jenny paused, waiting for any response the patient might make, but there was none.

Sophie Clary sat motionless, almost in a classic lotus pose, in the corridor outside the office. Jenny felt that the girl was aware of her presence, knew that someone was speaking to her, yet was unable to communicate in return.

People with schizoid tendencies were some of the most difficult people to nurse, and in Sophie's case this was compounded by her anorexia nervosa. She would eat a little, if coaxed gently, though generally on night duty this wasn't Jenny's problem.

Now it was Friday morning and past change-over time. A weary Jenny was longing for her bed, and fully intended to sleep the clock around. Breakfast was the day staff's problem, but Marie Thomson couldn't get Sophie to budge. For several hours she had been sitting there, hardly moving, seeming to want to be near Jenny. And, beyond seeing the girl was warmly wrapped up, Jenny had felt it wiser to leave her. She wouldn't come to any harm in the corridor, and a rota had been arranged, so that there was always a member of staff sitting with her.

Now, Jenny sank down beside her, talking to her gently, of nothing in particular. The question of breakfast wasn't mentioned, and she didn't urge Sophie to get up. Since the experienced Sister Thomson had met with resistance, there was no point in anyone else trying—not even Ben the Buccaneer.

Ben had stayed on the ward until nearly midnight.

Jenny frowned, as lost in introspection for a moment
as Sophie. There had been a phone call for him, which
came through to the ward. As luck would have it,
Jenny herself had picked up the phone, to hear a young
and rather husky female voice asking for Ben. 'Ben the
Buccaneer,' the voice had added, then laughed. It was
a decidedly sensual laugh, husky and warm-toned, and
dismaying to one Sister Fraser.

Ben had taken the call, his face wreathed in smiles,
when Jenny told him the caller was Carol. She then left
the office to begin yet another round of counting heads,
so that he shouldn't feel she was eavesdropping, but
she would have given a lot to know just who Carol
was!

Immediately he finished his telephone conversation,
Ben had wished Jenny a pleasant 'Goodnight', then
gone off duty, that disturbing smile lurking about the
corners of his mouth. Something had pleased him. Was
Carol waiting at home, warming his slippers by the
fire? Jenny wondered. Was she his wife? Someone
else's wife?

Questions and possible answers followed one
another in Jenny's mind, adding to her weariness.
Apart from Sophie's sit-in, the night was a quiet one,
except for Peggy Jefferson, who had decided to fly
again! Although Peggy's mood was more stable now,
she was still in the manic phase of her illness, and new
ideas or old ones suddenly recalled must be put to the
test straight away.

Jenny wished she could relate the story of the flight
to Sophie. Unfortunately, it wouldn't be in the girl's
best interests. The voices might latch on to the idea of
flying. No, it——

'Enjoying yourself down there, Sister?' a familiar
voice asked, and Ben Moran came striding along the
corridor. A happy, carefree Ben, Jenny noted. Evi-

dently he had enjoyed what remained of the night—
with Carol?

Dismayed by the strength of her feeling, Jenny
sought to rise. A large hand helped her up, Ben's hand
remaining under her elbow as they stood close
together. She wanted to pull away but knew it wouldn't
be wise. Ben would make her feel even more
uncomfortable if she did that. As it was, he must hear
the pounding of her heart, and certainly see the flush
that was inexorably creeping up her face. Damn the
man!

'Sophie——' she said quickly. 'She doesn't want to
move and I've been talking to her. Perhaps you can
persuade her?'

To Jenny's relief, Ben let her go, though his lips
quivered. He knew full well the effect he had on her!
Why didn't he stop tormenting her?

Ben hunkered down beside Sophie, who smiled.
'Good morning, Sophie. Can I ask you to move?' he
said gently, holding out his hand. 'They want to clean
the corridor and they can't while you're sitting there.
Come and sit in the dayroom.' Firmly he urged the girl
to her feet. Sophie didn't resist him, but nor did she
co-operate, simply allowing him to lead her away,
followed by Jenny.

They sat Sophie in the dayroom, arranged for a
nurse to sit with her, and to encourage her to eat when
the breakfast was brought in, then a tired Jenny
decided it really was time to call it a day.

'Quiet night?' Ben asked as they retraced their steps,
and Jenny shrugged.

'Reasonably. Anne stayed in all night and there was
no request to be let into the garden. Simon. . .' She
hesitated momentarily. 'He came to talk through his
problems, but I didn't let him stay long. Rachel is
concerned that he's half asleep by the time she gets to
see him, and I told him he must try to sleep at nights—

not during the day!' Yes, Simon was beginning to become a problem, though Jenny didn't intend confiding in Ben. It was something she had to work out for herself. 'Oh, and Peggy. That's why I was smiling to myself. She tried to fly last night. Well, around one o'clock, but we managed to dissuade her,' she finished laconically, and was warmed by Ben's chuckle.

'Now that I wish I'd seen! She told me she has to dance non-stop for twenty-four hours any time now as she's going to become a whirling dervish, but she hasn't mentioned flying for a few days,' Ben commented. 'I hoped her mood was coming down. Tell me about it,' he demanded, ushering Jenny into the interview-room.

Not wanting him to see how reluctant she was to be alone with him, Jenny sat down in a comfortable, low armchair and stretched out her legs clad in support stockings and sensible, low-heeled duty shoes. All of a sudden, she had the urge to discard her uniform and those ugly shoes, and slip into something cool, silky and sensual!

Wondering whether Carol was brunette, blonde or redhead, and deciding that she'd sounded like a sultry brunette, Jenny said, 'Is it an unbreakable rule that staff have to wear uniform? Rachel's job is rather different from ours, I know, but on an acute ward nurses often wear their own clothes. And what about calling them "clients"? That seems to be the trendy thing now.' She surveyed him from under half-closed lashes, her tired brain turning this way and that, unable to concentrate on anything for very long. Fatigue. She would have to be extra careful driving home.

Home? Hardly. A longing for a home of her own overcame her, as it often did when she was over-tired. A whole house, with a neat little garden in the front and a few fruit trees at the rear. And perhaps a terrace with white steps running down to the rear garden, as at Easterwood. Over by the meadow which marked the boundary, she could almost see the reflection of sunlight on the water. Yes, a pond, nothing more than that. Then there was that Martello tower. . .

She smiled drowsily, aware that Ben was watching her, but not caring very much. 'I'm half asleep,' she admitted. 'Sorry, Ben. My body clock hasn't adjusted to nights yet. I'm having difficulty in sleeping,' she added, though she hadn't meant to tell him. It really wasn't a problem for a consultant psychiatrist. It was reasonable to have a period of adjustment, as the body got used to working when it ought to be sleeping. Another week or two and she would be fine, if she could get *some* sleep. At the moment it was an elusive animal.

'A fatigued nurse isn't much use to the patients,' Ben said coldly. 'And no, I have no objection to nurses wearing their own clothes. That's something else we can have a meeting about! I'll drive you home—you can pick your car up any time it suits you.' He raised a hand as Jenny began feebly to protest. 'Don't argue, Sister Jenny. It's becoming a habit!'

'And being bossy and—opinionated and overbearing is becoming a habit with you!' she said unwisely. 'I'm fine and I *will* drive myself home. I'll see you next Monday.' With an effort, Jenny rose then stood gazing down at her stockinged feet. She hadn't been aware of removing her shoes.

'Neat little toes you have, Sister,' Ben commented, then held out his hand. 'Come on, *I'll* do the driving. I don't want any more accidents.'

Believing he spoke of Rachel, Jenny accepted gracefully. Although fiercely independent and resentful of 'the poor little woman' attitude among men, just this once, she decided, she would allow herself to be cosseted. It wasn't likely the opportunity would arise again!

All too soon, they arrived at her flat, and she

wondered whether it would be wise to invite her boss in. Yes, why not? Having decided that in her own mind, she was somewhat chagrined to find that he was keen to get away.

'Come on, out you get, Sister Jenny,' he said, opening the car door and helping her out. It wasn't the old Escort this time, it was a fairly new coupé, and Jenny had been enjoying the feel of real leather upholstery, the sheer luxury of feeling rich and pampered, the joy of being driven by the mesmerising Ben the Buccaneer. . .

No! She mustn't fall into that trap. She was a career woman—men were definitely out! 'I must have dozed off,' she murmured. 'Home at last. I can't wait to see my bed,' she went on, then was disconcerted to hear Ben's husky chuckle.

'I can't wait to see it, either,' he said softly; and Jenny turned on him, tiredness forgotten.

'That was a sexist remark, Dr Moran! And even if it was a joke, it's totally unacceptable!' she flashed.

Unabashed, he grinned at her. 'I never joke about the important things in life, Sister! I'll see you to the door, then I'll leave like a good little shrink, so don't be frightened.'

Before Jenny could think of a suitably cutting retort, Ben went on, 'Do I frighten you? I wonder. . .'

'Of course not,' Jenny said, glancing about her, aware that eyes from some of the other flats might be upon them. Here they were, a mature, professional man and woman, trading snide remarks in public like two schoolchildren! Her sense of humour came to the rescue, and she giggled. 'Sorry! We mustn't fight in public, Dr Ben. It isn't good for the image of psychiatry in the Nineties!'

'You're quite right, Sister. How about inviting me in for a coffee, instead? Then we can trade insults in private. No—you're asleep on your feet.'

'No, it's all right. I'll make you a coffee but——'

'But you change and fall into bed straight away. I remember now, you told me. Another time perhaps. I have to get home,' Ben added, dark eyes on her face.

'Yes, your wife will be expecting you. Thank you for the lift, Ben.' Jenny's voice faltered a little, but on the whole she was pleased with her performance. He had to get home, but to whom?

In silence, they climbed the stairs to her flat, and Ben waited while she got out her key. He took it from her trembling hand, fitted it into the lock, then pushed the door open for her. Then, as she turned to thank him, he flicked a finger against her cheek in a poignant gesture of farewell.

'Sleep well!' he called when he was halfway down the stairs, and Jenny smiled to herself without answering. She doubted very much whether she would sleep at all.

It was Saturday morning when she found the note which someone had slipped under her door. Not a note, really, just an expensive envelope containing a newspaper cutting, which she hurriedly thrust back, unread, into the envelope.

For a moment, her heart almost stopped beating. Memory of that other newspaper cutting came flooding back, the terse announcement that told her Lloyd had become her stepfather.

Realising how foolish she was being, but reluctant to read the cutting, Jenny left it on the chair by her bed until she dried her hair. There wasn't anything Lloyd and Angie could announce now. Although her mother was technically still fertile, Jenny doubted that she would wish for another child. Hadn't she been a mistake, bitterly regretted? Angie would be forty-five in July, Jenny mused idly, the hairdrier lying unused on her lap. No, the pleasures of motherhood wouldn't be welcome again.

The cutting probably wasn't from them at all. But who else would send her one? There was a photograph as part of the cutting, she had seen that much. She glanced apprehensively across at the envelope, which bore no name, and nothing to indicate who had sent it to her.

It was stupid leaving it lying there, unread. What possible harm could it do her?

Yet it was nearly two hours later that Jenny reluctantly decided that she must read it. In that time she had been shopping, picked up her car, washed out a few smalls, and generally done everything *but* open that intriguing envelope!

She smiled ruefully to herself as she unfolded the cutting, then wished she had left it unread. The head-lines from the local weekly paper thundered out at her: SHRINK'S WIFE IN HORROR SMASH! Stunned, she read on, after glancing at the date, which was the previous December—Christmas Eve, in fact.

> Police are appealing for witnesses after a horrific road crash left two dead and four people injured when a sports car and a van collided in icy conditions on the A21 just north of the junction with Hangley Cross. The accident, which happened in the early hours of yesterday morning, left both drivers dead. The passenger in the car, Mrs Louise Moran, wife of the prominent local psychiatrist, was cut out of the wreckage by firemen and taken to the general hospital with serious head injuries. The hospital described her condition as 'Critical but stable'. Dr Ben Moran, who remains at his wife's bedside in the intensive care unit, has declined to comment upon the accident. . .

The words jumped up and hit Jenny again and again, not heeding her cries of anguish. She felt physically sick as she relived the scene. Poor Louise. And poor, poor Ben.

The cutting went on to summarise Louise's work for local charities, but it was the name of her driver who caught Jenny's eye: Dean Bonner.

Rachel Bonner. Dean Bonner. The name wasn't particularly common—surely it wasn't just coincidence? Yet Rachel was divorced. This would make her a widow. And what was Mr Bonner doing travelling with Ben's wife at some unearthly hour? Unless. . .

Described as 'critical'. . . No way could Louise have survived a crash such as the one described. The accompanying picture was graphic proof of what had once been a car.

But what if she *did* survive? Poor Louise. 'It's my wife's birthday'—Ben's words last Tuesday.

Jenny scrutinised the cutting, seeking for words she had missed in her first hasty reading. It gave Louise's age, as those items always did. Thirty-nine. So last Tuesday Louise had been forty, the age at which life was said to begin.

Would have been forty, Jenny corrected herself automatically.

She sat staring into space for quite some time after that, the cutting carefully refolded and replaced in the envelope. Ben must have sent it to her, wanted her to know about his wife. Perhaps he did, indeed, live alone. But where exactly did Carol fit in?

She didn't feel like any lunch, but forced herself to prepare a poached egg on toast, then left it untasted, making fresh toast instead, and eating only half a slice. Ben needed comfort far more than she herself did. Lloyd was still alive. She had lost him but he still lived. Hers was a minor burden compared with the one Ben had shouldered, perhaps was still shouldering if Louise lingered on.

If Ben had turned to Carol for comfort, who could blame him? No, he had every——

The doorbell rang once, a long ring, then silence.

Jenny's eyes widened in dismay. It couldn't be Lloyd again, so it must be Ben. No one else would call on her at home.

Wondering how she would greet him in the light of this new knowledge, Jenny edged the door open, hoping it was a double-glazing salesman, or another woman selling fire extinguishers, anyone except Ben the Buccaneer!

Her wish was partly answered. Rachel Bonner stood outside the flat, her finger poised above the bell again.

They stared at each other for a long moment, then Jenny smiled. 'This is a surprise! Come in. I've been out shopping and I was thinking about having an after-lunch coffee. Will you have one?'

She led the way into the kitchen, where she had been sitting with her half-slice of toast. 'Not much of a lunch, by the looks of it,' Rachel commented, as she perched on the kitchen stool, resting her elbows on the brightly coloured breakfast bar. Her eyes followed Jenny around the room. 'Nice. It's bigger than my kitchen. I suppose it's rented, though?'

It was the sort of question that required no answer, and Jenny was irked. 'Yes, I rent it, but I'm looking around for a place to buy. Prices here are sky-high, though.'

'Not after London, surely? Of course, it *is* dear here,' Rachel purred, her mind obviously elsewhere. 'Look, about that cutting——'

Jenny whirled around. 'You sent it? I thought perhaps Ben had.'

'No! Do you think he wants everyone to know?' Rachel gave a short laugh. 'Of course, everyone *does* know. At the Easterwood, I mean. Except newcomers like yourself.'

Silence hung heavily between them, before Jenny nodded. 'Yes, I can see he wouldn't want to shout it from the roof-tops. Poor Ben. And poor Louise,' she went on quickly. 'What happened to her? Surely she isn't still alive?'

Rachel glanced down at her elegant, red-tipped fingernails before shaking her head. 'They put her on a life-support machine, but her injuries were dreadful. . . She never regained consciousness. That's one blessing, I suppose.'

'Where does your husband fit in? I thought you told me you were divorced.'

Rachel's eyes met hers, then slid away. 'We were divorced, but only just. If it hadn't been for Louise, Dean would have come back to me! I know he would!'

There was nothing Jenny could say to that. Words of comfort were so inadequate that she didn't even bother. Instead, she finished making the coffee, and pushed a beaker across to the therapist. 'Here. Would you like a biscuit? They're in that tin.' She pointed, but Rachel shook her head.

They drank in silence, though Jenny's mind was whirling with questions. Louise and Dean Bonner were having an affair, but why should Rachel want *her* to know that? If Ben preferred his tragedy to be kept secret, it was wrong of Rachel to send that cutting. Ben would be so hurt. . .

'Ben would be hurt if he knew,' she spoke her thought aloud.

'Then don't tell him,' Rachel said shortly. 'I sent it so you would know—about Ben and me, I mean. Louise took my husband, so I'm taking hers! Ben and I love each other, but it isn't a year yet. He has to think of his public image. It wouldn't do. . .' Rachel glanced sideways at her, as if wondering how she was taking the news.

In fact, it didn't come as the shock Rachel perhaps hoped. Really, it was obvious they cared for each other. But where did Carol come in? It was on the tip of Jenny's tongue to ask, but she deemed it wiser not to. Maybe Rachel didn't know about the other woman, and if Ben could enjoy a few moments of forgetfulness in the arms of Carol then Jenny wished him luck. Rachel wasn't right for him, but a man in love wouldn't see that.

'When will you announce the engagement?' Jenny kept her voice level, her expression no more than slightly interested, and Rachel frowned, as if unsure of her.

'After Christmas, probably. Or perhaps a little before.' She rose unhurriedly. 'I must be getting on, but I wanted you to know about Ben and me. He's such a handsome hunk that all the women fall for him, and I could see it happening to you, Jenny. You're too nice a person to be hurt again. I think you've been hurt before,' Rachel added perceptively.

'Is it that obvious? Yes, my fiancé married someone else,' Jenny admitted, without going into further details. 'And no, I'm not falling for Ben. The pain's too recent—I'm still picking up the pieces from last time!'

'I'm glad. There's no reason why we shouldn't work well together, is there? Enjoy your weekend.'

Rachel departed in a cloud of heavy perfume, which lingered until Jenny threw open all the windows. She leaned out as far as she safely could, breathing in the clean, fresh air, her heart heavy. Yet it was obvious that Ben loved Rachel. Hadn't she seen that from the very first day? Poor Louise, who hadn't, perhaps, been loved at all.

Jenny, who couldn't cry for herself, found tears on her cheeks as she cried for Ben's wife.

CHAPTER TEN

'JENNY! Wait for me!'

Startled, Jenny turned from her contemplation of
the Easterwood lake to see the neat figure of Babs
Richardson hurrying along. This time the secretary was
wearing a skirt of average length yet still contrived to
look like a figure from the Edwardian heyday of the
house.

'I'm glad you could come! Didn't I say how busy we
are on Sundays?' Babs exclaimed, her welcome warming Jenny.

They had met in the village when Jenny was out
shopping the previous day, and Babs had urged her to
take a fresh look at Easterwood now that she was
beginning to settle in. Sundays were always lively days,
Babs had insisted, and there were usually loads of
visitors.

She was proved right. Nearly everyone had a visitor,
and Jenny couldn't help contrasting it with her previous
hospital where only the recently admitted acute
patients had visitors on a regular basis.

'I never realised just how big the lake was,' Jenny
commented as she and Babs strolled by. Two rowing-
boats and a punt were doing a roaring trade as the
more hardy took to the water on the cool spring day.

'We make people pay but the money goes to a
different charity each month,' Babs was explaining.
'This time it's for the dogs. Next month it will be for a
children's charity, and in high summer the disabled
folk get their turn. Louise did a lot for the disabled,'
the secretary prattled on, as they skirted the southern-
most tip of the lake, and crossed the pretty rustic

bridge which led to a summer-house Jenny hadn't seen before.

Louise. Jenny badly wanted to ask about her, yet could not. It might get back to Ben. No, the subject of Louise must remain *verboten*.

'It's their flag day next Saturday. The local association for the disabled, I mean. Are you coming to sell flags?' Babs eyed her speculatively.

Surprised, Jenny agreed. 'I haven't been asked, but, yes, I'll come along. I've never been much good at flag-selling, though, so be warned!'

'I can't think why. You're pretty and blonde. That's always a help!' Babs paused to let a short, plump little girl come up with them.

'Hello, I'm Nazlin Arifuddin. Are you a visitor?' the child asked Jenny, who shook her head.

'I work here. With Dr Ben and your father.'

'I like Dr Ben,' Nazlin confided. 'He said he wished I was *his* little girl. He said he wanted my brothers and sisters to be his, too. Are you a mummy?'

This last remark was accompanied by a look of such eloquent pleading that Jenny felt mean. 'I haven't any children at all, I'm afraid. Are there many of you?'

Nazlin began to count on her fingers. 'We're five at present, though my big brother's at university so we don't count him. He's going to be a doctor, too. Mummy's over there. I'll tell her you want me to be your daughter. Perhaps Dr Ben will give you a daughter,' she added innocently, and Jenny felt her face grow hot.

Babs chuckled as the child ran off. 'Delightful children. Mine are all grown up now, I'm afraid, so I share the Arifuddin brood! Ben loves children,' she added, apparently as an afterthought, but Jenny refused to take the bait.

She glanced into the summer-house as they passed,

then turned back. Sophie Clary was sitting there, quite alone.

'Excuse me, Babs, I have to talk to Sophie. Does she have visitors?'

'Only her mother. She hasn't any friends. That sort of person never does. I don't think her mother's coming today. Take her for a walk—you might bump into Ben.' With a wave, she strolled on towards a group of visitors, leaving Jenny free to do what she liked best— talk to patients.

Sophie seemed unaware that she was no longer alone until Jenny touched her lightly on the arm. 'Sophie, it's Sister Jenny. You're cold, dear.'

The girl glanced up at last, then smiled, those beautiful turquoise eyes lighting up. 'Hello, Sister Jenny. No, I don't feel cold. Do you? Have you come far?'

Before Jenny could respond, one of the students came puffing up, two ice-cream cornets in her hand. 'Sorry, Sister! I left Sophie by the donkeys but she walked off. Here.' She handed a cornet to the patient, who stared down at it before tentatively beginning to eat.

Indicating to the nurse that she would take over her duties for the time being, Jenny sat down beside Sophie and stroked her hand, trying to warm it a little. The ice was licked once more without any noticeable pleasure, then Sophie dropped it neatly into the litter bin beside her.

'Haven't you any visitors today?' Jenny asked gently.

'No visitors today,' the girl intoned. 'They wouldn't let her come. They keep telling me she can't come today,' she went on sadly, but Jenny didn't know whether she meant the clinic authorities, or the imaginary voices.

Then a movement in the doorway caught her eye, and a casually dressed Ben Moran stepped across the

threshold, his hand outstretched towards Sophie. 'Time
you were back inside the house, Sophie.'

Obediently Sophie rose, then held out her hand to
Jenny. 'This is my visitor. They told me she couldn't
come today, but she has!'

Jenny and Ben exchanged glances. 'You're a lucky
girl. Some folk don't have visitors at all. We'll all go
up to the house and have a sticky bun,' Ben announced.

So, with Ben leading the way, they trooped out of
the summer-house, Jenny walking arm in arm with
Sophie. They didn't cross the bridge, Ben turning
instead towards a footpath Jenny wouldn't have seen.
This ran through a stretch of coppiced wood. Then,
through the trees, Jenny could see Easterwood. The
white building seemed to shimmer as they cut through
the trees and came out by the rose bower.

'It's beautiful from here,' Jenny breathed. 'It's the
sort of house people dream of owning,' she went on,
forgetting for a moment that it had once belonged to
Ben's family.

'You're not after Easterwood, are you? I thought
your mind was fixed on owning a Martello tower!'
Ben's laughter floated back as he lengthened his stride,
and they had to run to keep up with him.

The exercise warmed Sophie and brought a glow to
her cheeks, as well as to Jenny's. Hopefully it would
also bring on an appetite. Certainly a delicious smell of
baking wafted out to them from the kitchen as Ben
entered the house through what looked like a stable
door. This led to a huge, flagstoned scullery then into
a lobby, the kitchen itself being to one side. Jenny
glimpsed two figures busy at work in the kitchen, then
they passed through the green baize door to the living
quarters of the house.

'We'll sit in here,' Ben said firmly as Sophie seemed
inclined to wander off by herself. 'Here' proved to be
a room Jenny had glimpsed only briefly on her original

visit to the clinic. Medical magazines were strewn casually everywhere, and there were several book-shelves laden with enough books to warm the heart of any bookworm, herself included.

A large settee, covered in blue and cream striped silk, held pride of place in front of an open hearth, and Sophie made unerringly for this, stretched herself out, then lay with her back to the room, her head comfort-ably pillowed on one of the silk cushions.

Ben gave the girl a quick glance, then ran long fingers through his already disordered hair. 'I'll see what I can rustle up by way of food. I could eat an ox!'

Jenny laughed, despite her feeling of awkwardness. Of course he couldn't know about the newspaper cutting Rachel had given her. No, the awkwardness was all on her side. Knowing about Louise had altered her perception of him. She wished now she hadn't mentioned his wife so many times. How she must have hurt him! Yet why didn't he tell her?

'Jenny?' Ben shot her a puzzled look, and she coloured faintly.

'It's nothing. Roast oxen would be fine. Thank you,' she murmured, and he chuckled.

The door closed behind him, leaving Jenny feeling absurdly lonely. Left to herself, if one discounted the now silent Sophie, she went on a tour of the big room.

Like most of the rooms at the Easterwood, it had a high moulded ceiling. Here, too, were more of the ornate wood carvings, and her attention was caught by a particularly intricate piece of carving over a doorway at the far end of the room. It depicted a tiny bird with long tail feathers, its sharp beak stabbing at a tendril of what looked like honeysuckle. The carving was so lifelike that the eyes seemed alive, and each tail feather was so carefully and lovingly carved that Jenny almost expected the strange bird to take flight.

Her curiosity aflame now, she sought for more of the

carvings. Although there were smaller ones in the room, these were mainly of flowers and she found nothing like the bird. Over the mantelpiece there was a depiction of grapes with pieces of foliage, and, lower down, more of the honeysuckle, but her gaze kept returning to the bird.

Then the main door was opened and Ben came in with a laden tray.

'Here we are, folks—chow's up!' he announced with a wide grin, and Jenny moved swiftly to bring up a small table.

'It looks good and it smells good,' she commented.

'By heaven, it *is* good!' he finished for her, and she half turned towards Sophie, not wanting to share Ben's laughter. She had no right to it.

Sophie proved obstinate, which wasn't unexpected, and Ben left a large plate by the settee. On it he placed a warm, crusty roll liberally spread with butter, a small pasty, and an apple. The size of the plate made the small portion look even smaller, and Sophie might be deceived into thinking she could eat everything on it without gaining pounds in weight.

The fear of gaining weight, of becoming round and fat, was a constant factor in anorexia nervosa, and in Sophie's case her serious mental disorder made it so much worse. Possibly the voices told her everything she ate was poisoned, Jenny mused as she sat in one of the matching armchairs and accepted the plate Ben handed her. She had no such fears, and tucked into two of the crusty rolls and some fruit before pronouncing herself full.

She licked a dab of butter from her lips, aware that Ben's eyes were following the movement, then hastily she bit into another apple. 'I won't need anything else today. Thank you, Dr Ben,' she said, her eyes lowered over the fruit.

Ben rose, then yawned and stretched, big muscles

straining against the old shirt he wore. He was in black today, Jenny noted, and it suited him. All he needed was a gaily coloured scarf tied round his head and a cutlass stuck into the wide leather belt he wore!

Laughing and eating at the same time caused her to cough, and it was the buccaneer himself who came over to gently pat her back, his touch doing extraordinary things to her heartbeat.

'Sorry! I was—was just thinking all you needed was a cutlass tucked in your belt!' Jenny tried to rise but Ben pushed her down gently.

'Take your time. People can die like that, you know. Here.' He held out a spotlessly clean linen handkerchief. Then, before she could grasp it, he dabbed at her mouth, which was still shiny from the butter.

His touch unnerved her, yet he was doing no more for her than he would do for a patient. It could be Sophie sitting here being the recipient of the psychiatrist's TLC. It could be, but it wasn't. It was one Sister Jenny Fraser who sat immobile, like a frightened little wild creature.

'Thank you, Dr Ben,' she forced herself to say calmly, when he sat back, his face expressionless. 'That was a silly thing to do. Wasn't it, Sophie?' Out of the corner of her eye, Jenny had seen the patient stirring.

Now Sophie sat up, ignoring them both but picking up the roll and beginning to pull minute pieces out of it. When there were several on the plate she began to eat them, while Jenny and Ben pretended not to notice.

'I was wanting to ask you about the wood carvings, Ben,' Jenny said, as Sophie paused halfway through the roll. 'They're so lifelike! They're too recent for Grinling Gibbons, so who carved them?'

Ben got up again and strolled over to the other door, gazing up at the carvings, his broad back to her.

Jenny moved her hands restlessly in her lap as she fought down the urge to rush up and wrap her arms around him, run her hands up and down his spine, breathe in the fragrance of his hair, feel the passion rising between them as his head bent to hers, his mouth crushing all resistance. . . . A small sigh escaped her, and she tensed. But Ben was speaking and could not, thankfully, have heard.

'I think Gibbons would have been proud to think they *were* his work, though. No, it was Joshua Moran, one of my many relatives,' he said, pride in his voice.

Seeing that Sophie had resumed eating, Jenny joined Ben by the door, being careful to keep just out of touching distance. The tide of desire was still strong within her, and Ben must surely pick up the vibrations.

He pointed to the intriguing fan-tailed bird, seemingly unaware of the battle Jenny was fighting with herself. 'That's unlike any bird I've seen. It looks tropical—perhaps some kind of bird of paradise,' he went on musingly. 'Josh hadn't been out of England then, and I doubt that he'd ever had the opportunity to look at plates in natural history books. He was one of the poor relations that folk took into their homes in those days.'

Was there just a trace of bitterness in his voice? Jenny wondered. 'You aren't going to tell me he had no formal training?'

'That's just what I am going to tell you! Not only that, he had no formal education, either. Since he was a poor relation, I guess they didn't bother too much about schooling him. Why should they?' Ben demanded. 'Yet, somehow, he was able to develop this wonderful talent. The family had a handyman who carved wood as a sideline, and he encouraged the boy.'

Ben stood back a little, the better to admire the carvings. 'He did all the carvings you'll find in the house, but that's the only bird. The only living creature, come to that—all the rest are flowers and fruit. He called it the *Bird of Hope*.'

Surprised, Jenny moved nearer. 'What happened to him?' she asked quietly, not wanting to distroy the spell Ben's unknown ancestor had thrown over them both. A feeling of peace, of contentment, came over her, in sharp contrast to her previous far-from-peaceful feelings! And when Ben glanced down and smiled into her eyes, Jenny wanted nothing more to complete her happiness.

Sophie broke the spell, and Jenny realised it was just as well, for who knew where that moment of togetherness might have taken them?

'I've eaten it all, Dr Ben. May I go now?' Sophie asked politely.

'Yes, you can go, Sophie. Sister Jenny will take you back upstairs. About Josh——' Ben hesitated a moment, then shrugged. 'He went away. He just upped and took off one day.'

Jenny took Sophie back to the ward, then made her way on to the terrace. The sun was hiding behind some ominous-looking clouds by now, and most of the visitors had dispersed. She greeted one or two of her own patients who were making their way up to the house for tea, Ivy Millington among them.

Miss Millington looked slightly ashamed as she met Jenny's speculative glance, and hesitated before moving across to speak to her. 'I'm sorry about Stella, Sister. I suppose I should have told you but I knew she was safe. If she hadn't been——' Miss Millington broke off awkwardly, and Jenny took pity on her.

'It's all right, Miss Millington. You felt you couldn't betray her confidence, but please tell us in future,' Jenny pleaded. 'We had people out all night searching, and I was worried sick! Have you heard from her?'

'Yes, she rang me this morning. I think she feels she ought to come and apologise to you personally, but. . .'

'If she wants to come back, just for a short visit, I'll be glad to see her. No one will try to prevent her leaving, if that's a worry to her,' Jenny assured the woman. 'Nor do I expect an apology—but I would like to know how she got out.' Jenny felt that Anne Bomford would figure in the solution somewhere. Ben had held an informal enquiry but no member of staff would admit to having let Stella Lawrence out, and Anne herself hadn't asked for the door to be unlocked.

'Well, I promised Stella. . .'

'If there's a way out of the clinic that we don't know about, then you really ought to tell us,' Jenny said forcefully. 'If Sophie were to discover it and run off, I'm sure you would feel guilty. So would Mrs Lawrence,' she pointed out, wishing that Ivy Millington didn't have such a strongly developed sense of duty!

'Yes, you're right, but there's no chance of Sophie getting out that way. I'll phone Stella tomorrow and ask her if I may tell you.' And, with that, a flustered but determined Miss Millington hurried into the house, leaving Jenny feeling more alone than ever.

'You're ready to do battle with someone, Jenny!' Ben's amused voice broke in on her thoughts, and she whirled around as he joined her on the terrace. 'Did I see you with Ivy Millington?' At Jenny's surprised nod, Ben went on, 'I've already pointed out the error of her ways. I told her it was very commendable of her to be so loyal to her friend, but that we needed to know about any loopholes in the security.' He chuckled. 'I told her we didn't want any of our patients *or* nurses ravished on the premises!'

'I hope your words had more force than mine,' Jenny said feelingly. 'I can understand her not wanting to betray a confidence, but surely she realises the dangers?'

'I doubt it. Anyway, I've been doing a little detective work,' Ben confessed, taking her arm as they strolled back inside the house. 'I've been over every inch of this place and I'd stake my reputation on it that there's no way anyone can get in *or* out.'

Jenny, her nerves all a-twitter, was prepared to belive him, but as their steps led them inexorably back to the *Bird of Hope* room her mind was fully concentrated upon ways of extricating herself.

'It's my guess it's human error—or a human a certain Anne Bomford has managed to charm,' Ben went on, apparently unaware of her turmoil. 'There's one member of staff I still have to interview, a junior night porter. He's gone sick, conveniently. Wouldn't you say it was convenient, Sister Jenny?'

He turned to her, his eyes warm, but Jenny didn't trust herself to speak. This was ridiculous! She was behaving like a young girl out on her first date. There was definitely no reason for her to feel hot and bothered, apprehensive even.

'You're too young for hot flushes. That wouldn't be a blush, now would it?'

Jenny's colour deepened, then the air suddenly became charged with a powerful force that neither could control. Ben reacted instinctively. Without thinking, he enfolded Jenny in his strong, caring embrace, his tender kisses finding her forehead, her cheeks. Finally he lowered his mouth to hers and almost reverently kissed her sweet lips.

'Oh, Jenny, my——' Just in time, Ben bit back the word 'darling'. She loved someone else, someone who had hurt her, just as he would have to hurt her. His head might reason it out sensibly, but his heart told him differently, and he crushed her closer to him, his hands roving caressingly over her body, feeling the heat of her through the thin sweater she wore.

When they stopped to draw breath, Jenny was almost sobbing with the pent-up emotion which had been released so dramatically. She tried to speak but her throat was full of tears. Without conscious thought, she lifted her tear-stained face for another kiss, just one final kiss. But it was to be denied her. Instead, Ben ran his tongue over her eyelids and down her cheeks, erasing the tears as they fell. Then he kissed the tip of her nose before releasing her.

Jenny felt chilled, bereft without the warmth of his arms. One part of her mind was on that half-open door. Anyone could have seen them. It was a crazy thing to do in a house full of people, yet it felt so right!

'Jenny, I——' Ben began, but a loud knock on the door stopped her from hearing what might have been an apology. Anne Bomford stood there, her astute gaze going from one to the other.

'Sorry to bother you, but you've got a visitor, Dr Ben!' she announced, with a big grin. 'Here she is!' She stood aside to let a short, willow-slender brunette enter.

'Carol!'

'Ben the Buccaneer!'

So this was the mysterious Carol! So much for the dreams of Sister Jenny Fraser. Her lips still burned from Ben's kisses, but it didn't matter. She would get over it. In fact, she prided herself that she was becoming something of an expert now. She might even give free lectures to an enthralled audience on the subject of patching up a broken heart.

CHAPTER ELEVEN

WEDNESDAY night was another quiet night at
Easterwood. So far, anyway, Jenny amended as she
headed towards Peggy Jefferson's room. They had
been lonely nights, too, and she missed one Benjamin
Moran more than she was prepared to admit, even to
herself.

He hadn't, she noted, appeared on nights since the
arrival of Carol Smithson—*Dr* Carol Smithson. The
young and engaging Carol had proved to be a GP
trainee who was to spend six months at the Easterwood
as her post-basic training in psychiatry. She was in her
twenties and far too young for Ben, of course, but. . .

Just in time Jenny changed the direction of her
thoughts. Carol was her own age or no more than a
year younger, so they were both too young for the
consultant psychiatrist.

When she reached Peggy's room, which was a single
room to reduce the external stimuli, the woman was
sitting up in bed staring at the wall and reciting to
herself.

'Peter Piper picked a peck; a bushel and a peck;
down came a blackbird and pecked off her her nose;
noses, roses; roses are red——'

'Shouldn't you be asleep, Peggy?' Jenny asked
gently, and the patient eyed her resentfully.

'I've been asleep. Now I'm awake. I'd like my
breakfast now. Now is the hour,' she went on, 'I've
been awake for hours and hours. And——' Evidently
finding nothing to associate with 'hours', Peggy
stopped, then began again just as Jenny tried to settle
her down in the bed. 'Tomorrow is another day, hours

and minutes gone forever, another day we've thrown
away. Away in a manger——'

Hours and minutes gone forever, another day we've
thrown away. How right Peggy was! Leaving her to her
aimless punning, Jenny headed for the clinic. Ben
hated medicating anyone and held strong views about
nurses who, because they couldn't cope with a particular patient's behaviour, went overboard and gave all
the medication which had been written up. But, in
Peggy's case, she certainly needed more for her own
sake.

'On the warpath, Jenny?' Simon Jenkins materialised
out of the shadows.

'You'll have to be like Peggy, sing a little song or
even whistle so I know you're there,' Jenny said, more
sharply than she had intended. 'You startled me—can't
you sleep, either?'

'The office door was closed before, then I heard
Lesley laughing and I wished I could join in,' Simon
said wistfully. 'I thought everyone was in there having
a good time. Then I saw Staff in the sitting-room with
some of the ladies, so I knew *she* hadn't deserted us.'

'None of us has deserted you, but when it's quiet I
like to teach the students. And Lesley, too, of course.
Are there any problems? No one else wandering
about?' Simon had appointed himself her bodyguard at
nights, and certainly was able to alert her if anything
untoward happened. It did at least take his mind off
his problems.

Simon shook his head. 'I was wondering. . .' He
hesitated. 'I know you sometimes go shopping for the
ladies when you're off. Could I come with you one
afternoon?'

'I can't see any reason why not, but only if it doesn't
interfere with your therapy,' Jenny hedged. 'I go home
to sleep first but I could meet you in the town after

lunch?' she sugested, and Simon's dejected expression vanished as he enthusiastically agreed.

Jenny realised that Rachel wouldn't approve, but wasn't prepared, the following morning, for Ben's reaction to the idea. He had just arrived when she hesitantly mentioned taking Simon shopping. The sun was already up, and the ward was all bustle as patients got themselves washed and dressed.

'Do you think that's wise?' was all he said, but instantly Jenny bristled.

'If he needs to go shopping, I can't see any reason against it,' she said defiantly.

'Of course not, but Simon's a married man and perhaps it isn't helpful for him to be out in the town with another woman. His wife could see you, and,' Ben went on, as Jenny opened her mouth to protest, 'we need to get away from patients' problems when we're off duty. If you encourage him to use you as——'

'I'm not encouraging him to do anything!' Jenny said, stung. 'If I reject him, more or less say, "Sorry, you're a psychiatric patient, I don't want to be seen out with you," what will that do to him?'

'Don't take that line with me!' Ben snapped back, astonishing both of them. His colour was raised, and he looked more the pirate than ever as he glared down at Jenny.

'I'm sorry, Doctor,' Jenny said quietly, 'but what I do in my off-duty time is my own affair. Just as what you do is yours,' she added, thinking of Carol. Of course, now she knew who Carol was she could understand their spending time together, but that didn't make it any easier to bear.

'I see,' was all Ben said, his anger disappearing as suddenly as it had arisen, but Jenny was aware that he saw too much!

'What I mean is,' she hastened on, 'I can see your

point, but since Simon asked me I can't refuse, as long as it doesn't interfere with his treatment. If Rachel needs him on the ward, then I'll have to explain that perhaps a Saturday would be more appropriate.' Jenny's breathing was faster, her own colour heightened, and she felt like screaming and crying both at once. If only she could make Ben see! What it was she wanted to make him see she wasn't entirely sure, but funnily enough Carol Smithson was there somewhere in her muddled thoughts.

'I suggest we leave it to Rachel to make the decision,' Ben was saying. 'If she disapproves, it could be that you need to think again, even about Saturdays. By the way, Stella's husband phoned me last evening. Stella's coming back to see you tonight.'

'I'm glad,' Jenny said warmly. 'Perhaps she'll make up her mind to return. We have a vacancy—can she have it?'

'I think wait a while, see how she gets on at home. She's driving her husband crazy, and when he's driven *too* far she might decide to come back and try to co-operate more with her therapy.'

Ben left her to pull all the threads of the night shift together, then go off duty. Only one more night, then she was free—certainly free of Ben.

Cursing the fate that had brought her to Sussex in general, and to the Easterwood in particular, Jenny got into her car and headed back to the loneliness of her flat. She must, she decided, take up some absorbing hobby, pursue an outside interest, just as she advised patients to do. Perhaps the flag day would distract her attention from the incurable symptoms of unrequited love!

'How are we doing?' Simon asked, and Jenny rattled her collecting tin experimentally.

'Not too well. It's eleven flags, isn't it? I've been

trying to keep count but buyers are coming so thick
and fast, it's a job!' she quipped. As it was raining,
with a stiff breeze blowing, it was hardly surprising
they weren't doing so well. Then a sudden gust of wind
caught her jaunty tasselled cap, and Simon set off in
pursuit.

Selling flags could hardly be called a hobby, yet it
was just what Jenny needed, and she had firmly put
Ben the Buccaneer from her mind. Simon, too, was
benefiting from doing something useful, an activity
which didn't cause pressure. Most of the clinic staff
were collecting in the town, but so far there was no
sign of Ben or Rachel.

Jenny glanced about for Simon, who had vanished,
tasselled cap and all, then lost interest in him as a
couple approached—Ben with Dr Carol!

'You look as though you could eat a hot lunch,' Ben
commented. 'Would you care to join us? Or are you
chained to the spot for another hour?'

'We're staying until twelve. Then I thought we might
change our venue. Simon's gone in search of my cap,'
Jenny explained to Carol Smithson.

'Mm, yes, Ben saw him talking to a rather muscular
young woman who turned out to be his wife! She was
nagging him when we passed,' Carol went on, pulling a
face.

Jenny's startled gaze went to Ben. 'Should we rescue
him, do you think? Mrs Jenkins might undo all the
good we've done!' Her big eyes pleaded for advice, for
understanding, though she wasn't conscious of it, and
Ben wanted to kiss the tip of her little pink nose, rub
some warmth into her hands, hold her against his heart
and kiss her so thoroughly that she wouldn't have a
chance to draw breath. And all he could do was discuss
the pros and cons of letting Simon's wife nag him!

'I don't think we should interfere, Jenny—a little
nagging won't do Simon any permanent harm. Where's

my flag?' Ben asked, and a flustered Jenny peeled off one of the blue stickers and pressed it against the lapel of his jacket. Her hand trembled slightly, but she thought she did rather well to control her feelings. But Ben and Carol! Where did that leave Rachel? she wondered miserably.

'I'll have a word with Simon, if you like,' Ben offered, 'then we'll be on our way. I have a busy afternoon.' He hurried off, leaving the two women together, with neither knowing quite what to say.

Carol's eyes were understanding as they rested upon Jenny. 'Ben's got to see a patient this afternoon, but we won't be getting him at the Easterwood. People under Section go to the unit at the general, Ben tells me.'

'Yes, so I gather. It's hard enough persuading the informal ones to stay without having people legally confined! Did Ben tell you a patient walked out one night recently? On *my* shift,' Jenny added.

Carol shrugged. 'People have free choice. If they don't want to be helped, they can't be. It's like alcoholics,' Carol went on, then continued on what seemed to be her pet subject. 'Wouldn't you agree?' she said, and Jenny gathered her thoughts together, trying to remember exactly what Carol had been saying, but Ben and Simon were coming towards them, and Simon was visibly shaking.

'Did you bring my hat?' she asked, deciding to ignore Simon's attack of nerves.

'Oh, no! I picked it up then I must have put it down again.' He glanced about him helplessly, then at Ben, who produced her crumpled scarlet cap from his pocket.

'Doctor to the rescue,' Ben proclaimed, setting it on Jenny's fair hair and tugging it down over her ears to keep them warm. His hands stayed a fraction longer

than was necessary, and Jenny, out of the corner of her
eye, saw Carol's shrewd glance.

'Thank you, Dr Ben,' Jenny said primly, then rattled
her tin. 'I don't know about Simon, but I'm beginning
to think I'm invisible!' Please say something innocuous,
Ben, she silently pleaded. Talk about flags, doing good,
anything at all, but don't look at me like that.

'I think,' Carol said slowly, 'that we should leave
Doctor and Night Sister to a discussion on flag-selling.
Let's go in search of a cup of coffee, Simon, shall we?
I'll be coming to work at the Easterwood and you can
fill me in on the routine.' With that, Carol led a
protesting Simon away towards the town centre, leaving Jenny alone with Ben. Carol's kindness was appreciated but misplaced. There was nothing they could say
to each other.

Ben prised the roll of flags from her fingers, then
stood beside her while she held the collecting tin aloft.
It was cruel of him to stand within touching distance.
Yet she couldn't, mustn't, touch him. She realised
there probably wasn't anything between him and Carol,
but there was no doubt they were good friends and
might, eventually, become more than that. But there
was still Rachel Bonner. And still the shadow of
Louise, looming over them all, and perhaps she was
the greatest rival of all. Louise who did so much for
charity; Louise who was sadly missed by the local
people; and Louise who had died tragically while out
with another man.

'Jenny?' She became aware that Ben was speaking.
'Let's see if we can fill the tin.'

'What about your lunch date?' she asked in a small
voice, secretly pleased that he would remain by her
side a little longer.

'That's up to Carol,' he said shortly. 'She's got her
hands full with Simon. It's good practice for her.' He
paused to bestow a flag—and a charming smile—upon

another brave soul, then continued, 'You know about Louise.'

It was more statement than question, but Jenny didn't want to mention the newspaper cutting. Ben would be angry and hurt, and she couldn't bear that. 'Yes, someone said Louise died in an RTA. I wish you'd told me, not let me keep on about your wife expecting you——' She broke off as several more people came up. The weather was beginning to clear now and they were kept busy for a while, leaving them, thankfully, no privacy to resume their conversation. She didn't want to talk about Louise, and she rather thought Ben didn't, either.

'What about Simon?' she asked. 'Should I leave you in charge of the tin and go off to rescue Carol?'

'No!' Aware that he'd been too vehement, Ben went on quickly, 'He's had a pretty good drubbing by his wife. Let him talk to Carol. She's a new ear—he must have told you his entire life story by now. It will do him good to tell someone else.' And do Jenny good to be relieved of some of the strain Simon was putting on her. She was too caring a nurse, if that was possible, the sort who got easily exhausted, drained. He didn't want that to happen to her.

They had done rather well by the time Carol returned. Simon was, Jenny noted, talking animatedly to the young doctor. 'We've missed you, Simon,' she said, 'but we've sold all our flags and had to get another roll!'

Simon gave them a sour look. 'Great. Shall we get back to the Easterwood, Jenny? Dr Carol says she and our eminent friend here are lunching together.'

Jenny thought her 'eminent friend' gave Simon rather a jaundiced look but knew she must be mistaken. She had thought it wisest not to travel alone with Simon, and on the return journey, as on the outward one, Babs made up a threesome, her loquaciousness more noticable because Simon didn't contribute even the polite word or two he'd managed on the way to town. Jenny wondered what his wife had been saying. Although they were separated, she believed they might get back together once Simon was free of his symptoms.

Once they'd dropped Babs, Jenny drove Simon to the doors of Easterwood. 'How are you feeling now?' she asked carefully.

'I feel I've been set back at least six months!' he said bitterly, turning to her. 'It's that shrink! He had no right to send me off with Dr Carol! I wanted to stay with you—can't he see how important you are to me?'

There was such anguish in Simon's voice that Jenny couldn't think straight for a minute. Ben was right: it wasn't therapeutic for her to be seen with a male patient, not because other people might get the wrong idea, but because the patient himself had!

'You really don't know how much I adore you?' Simon said unsteadily, and Jenny shook her head. Then, for something to do, she pulled off her jaunty cap and held it defensively to her.

'Patients often fall for their nurses but it's an unnatural form of dependency. Just because Nurse does this for you, Nurse does that, male patients think how nice it would be to have Nurse around all the time. But it doesn't work, Simon! Anyway, I'm not free. I suppose you wouldn't realise that,' she finished slowly.

'Not free?' Simon echoed. 'Then it's true—what Anne said? You and Dr Ben?'

'No! Good heavens, where did you get that idea? No, there's someone else—from London. Naturally I don't talk about my private life,' she said unsteadily.

'Anne said she saw you—you and Dr Ben making love, and I called her a liar. *Is* she a liar, Jenny? Be honest with me, I can take it.' Although Jenny shook her head, her expression must have given her away. 'I see. That's that, then.'

He looked so dejected that Jenny longed to comfort him, but that would be as unwise as the kiss she and Ben had shared. And if Anne and Simon could see her love for Ben, who else might see it? Unwilling to be drawn into a discussion, she said instead, 'In you go and head straight for the dining-room, or you'll miss lunch altogether.'

With a wave for the patient, who didn't turn to acknowledge it, Jenny turned her car in the carriage sweep, wishing fervently that she had never come to the Easterwood psychiatric clinic. Yet that would mean wishing she had never met Ben the Buccaneer, and, no, she couldn't wish *that*, no matter how much heartache he had caused her.

She wasn't herself for the rest of that Saturday, but after phoning her grandmother and arranging to go up for her holiday in July she felt better. A change of scenery was what she needed, a chance to get her problems in perspective. Gran would stand no nonsense if she thought her only granddaughter was brooding!

Her best friend, a girl she'd trained with, was now nursing in the USA, and that was an idea Jenny had toyed with briefly. She had discarded the idea of applying because she hadn't wanted to be so far away from Lloyd. It was amazing, looking back, how much of her life he had taken. They'd been no more than acquaintances for months, then one day she realised he was the man she wanted to spend the rest of her life with, and they had become lovers. Perhaps Lloyd hadn't been as keen on marriage as she was, but he had proposed readily enough, and everything had been fine.

Then Angie had returned to London—Angie, with

her top job, her jet-setting way of life. Lloyd had been lost. Yet Angie, did she but know it, had done her only child a good turn. Jenny was free of Lloyd now. Free— only to fall under a stronger spell. Once more, she had fallen for a man she couldn't have.

Shrugging aside *all* her problems, she decided, later, to take a walk through the village which gave its name to the old house. Donning anorak and jaunty cap once more, she made her way to the small park which used to belong to Easterwood the house but was not used by Easterwood the village.

Someone else had the same idea, and she and Ben came face to face as she reached the main gates of the park. He had a Jack Russell in tow.

'Louise used to take her out. It's a chore I've taken on,' he said, with a wide grin, indicating the dog, who sniffed eagerly around Jenny's legs.

Jenny bent to stroke it, not wanting to meet Ben's gaze. Louise's good deeds again. Was there no end to them? she wondered. 'Exercising the dog is good for you, Doctor! I'm just on my way to the village.'

'Why? There's nothing there. The whole place is dead on a Saturday afternoon. Come and help me throw sticks for Suki here. Or I'll throw the stick and you can chase after it! She belongs to one of Louise's protégées,' Ben explained. 'Louise loved animals.'

Jenny's eyes were concerned as she glanced up at him, but she surprised an expression on his face which, had the circumstances been different, she might have thought was tenderness.

Dismissing such wishful thinking, the severely practical Sister Fraser decided she had seen enough of one Ben the Buccaneer for this weekend. 'I'll leave you to your dog-walking. See you next week, I expect!'

No, she couldn't spend more time with Ben, not without giving away her secret. Simon had guessed. How soon would it be before Ben did?

The village, though as quiet as Ben had described, was pretty, and in summer the cottage gardens would be a riot of flowers. There were even one or two thatched cottages at the northern end of Easterwood. And, when she had given in to the urge to follow a narrow, meandering footpath, she found the charming little church whose spire could be seen from the main street.

The church was an oasis of peace and serenity, and Jenny sat for a while in a pew near the back. Someone took care of it, for there were flowers and bits of greenery everywhere, many of the spring flowers she recognised as coming from the grounds of Easterwood.

To complete the picture of rural peace there was even a churchyard. Of course it probably hadn't seen a burial for years, but there was something restful in strolling along the paths and trying to decipher the grey, lichened gravestones. Then a thought struck her, and, intrigued, she perused every stone, but there were no Morans. She would have thought the local landed family might have been buried in the crypt of the church, yet had seen no plaques to that effect, either.

She straightened, becoming aware of being watched. Another Moran, a very much alive one, was gazing thoughtfully at her, and, feeling that she had intruded on a private preserve, she said, 'I was looking for Josh.'

'The wandering boy returning to be buried at home?' Ben took her hand and together they strolled back along the path. 'Josh lived to be ninety,' he went on. 'He came back for a while but he couldn't settle.'

'Was he your grandfather, Ben?' Jenny didn't need an answer, it was all becoming clear now. 'The poor relation made good, after all.'

'He certainly came back loaded,' Ben said with a smile. 'He brought a Greek bride back with him—my grandmother. My parents were English and I was born at Easterwood but the house never belonged to me. Or to Josh, come to that, no matter that Rachel seems to think I was deprived of my heritage! My folks went out to Australia to be with Josh, and my father still lives in Perth. The Moran who built the house died in Canada, and the rest left once Easterwood was sold.' He paused, his gaze searching. 'Suki couldn't wait to get back to her mistress, so that means I'm free now. How would you like me to open a few cans? Or cook some spaghetti?' he suggested with a malicious smile, and Jenny chuckled.

'Don't mention spaghetti to me! Yes, I would appreciate sampling the contents of a few cans,' she said rashly.

If she had given the matter proper thought, she would have found some plausible excuse for not accompanying Ben to his home. But then he might have accepted her refusal and taken someone else home, mightn't he? she told herself. No, whatever the dangers, she *wanted* to go home with Ben the Buccaneer.

CHAPTER TWELVE

IF JENNY had thought about Ben's home at all, she would have visualised floral curtains fluttering in the breeze, big windows with ruched nets, flowers everywhere, a woman's caring hand evident in every aspect of the home. If not Louise's hand, then someone else's. But this was definitely a bachelor pad, and she didn't know whether to be glad or sorry.

She had suspected that Ben didn't live alone, hadn't believed him when he said he got lonely at home, and had been consumed with jealousy as well as curiosity. Well, now she had her answer. If he did live with someone, she must be a colourless personality with no home-making talents!

Ben had left her in a big square room that was obviously kept for best. A water-colour hung on one wall, but there were no vases or ornaments anywhere. Even the small bookshelf was tidy, and, glancing at some of the titles, Jenny couldn't imagine that Ben ever read them; a book on bee-keeping kept company with an ancient-looking title on household etiquette. That, in turn, jostled with crochet for the beginner! Louise must have had wide interests, unless she collected second-hand books on impulse. Jenny decided that was probably the answer to the riddle—Louise had been a creature of impulse.

But what was Louise like, *really* like? There were no photographs to help Jenny to assess her character, no little gewgaws spread around the room to reflect her taste. Nothing. It was as if Louise had never been.

Tired and depressed by the spartan room, Jenny made her way along a narrow, carpeted passageway to the kitchen. This proved to be a much brighter room with a lived-in look. It was long and narrow, with an alcove at the far end for a small table and two stools. Ben stood by the stove, frowning over the directions on a packet of burger mix.

He turned at her approach and waved the packet. 'Vegetarian burgers. You make them up with water, but I don't seem to have the knack. There's a packet of mashed potato in the cupboard, and cans of tomato and peas in the floor cupboards. Will that do?' Ben's smile was lop-sided. 'I couldn't find any spaghetti bolognese,' he went on, 'but if that's what you'd *really* like, I can put it on my shopping-list for next week,' he offered.

'If you mention spaghetti bolognese ever again, I shall resign! Anyway, I'm not sure I want a burger just at the moment. A cup of tea and a biscuit would suit me fine,' Jenny assured him, though the pangs of hunger were beginning to unsettle her. Belatedly she remembered that she hadn't eaten since breakfast. After the events of the morning, food had been the last thing on her mind.

Ben looked pained. 'I wanted to show off my culinary prowess. Or yours.' He tapped the chest freezer. 'This is full to overflowing. We could have a real feast—if you'd care to do the honours?'

Jenny sighed. 'It looks as though I haven't any choice. I wondered why you were so eager to invite me home to dine!'

While Ben settled himself comfortably on one of the stools, Jenny set about making a scratch meal, and soon the aroma of grilled chops, sausages and tomatoes filled the room, and Ben sniffed appreciatively.

'You were lying to me, Sister Jenny—you *can* cook! I'll have to invite you more often.'

Jenny mistrusted that innocent expression, and shook her head firmly. Face flushed from the grill, she turned to give him a sour look. 'I'm a highly qualified nurse, I'll have you know. *I* wasn't put on this earth to slave after some man!'

'Now you're going to call me a selfish, chauvinistic swine,' he sighed, and she couldn't help laughing.

'That's exactly what you are, Dr Ben! If you *could* lower yourself sufficiently to lay the table, we can eat.'

Ben did, at least, express his appreciation of the meal, so honours were even. 'It's very pleasant to have someone to cook for me. Thank you, Jenny.' At her raised brow, he went on, 'Did I say something out of place?'

'No, it's just that——' She hesitated. Really, it was none of her business. Didn't *she* object to others prying into her private life? 'I find it hard to believe a man as attractive and handsome as yourself can't find anyone to cook for him. With all the food in that fridge and freezer, you can't expect me to believe you really live alone!'

'No, I don't expect you to believe that,' Ben said, after a moment. 'Though, as I'm so well-known here, keeping a live-in lover might prove kind of difficult. Wouldn't you say?'

'Yes. I'm sorry, I didn't think. Anyway, it's not my affair,' she said brightly, and Ben's smile was sad. No, it wasn't Jenny's affair, just as *her* private life was no business of his. That was a great pity.

After their meal, they moved to a room at the back of the house. Ben threw open the door and announced, 'This is Ben's den!'

Ben's den was in sharp contrast to the sitting-room and bore the stamp of his own personality. It was a masculine room for a thoroughly masculine man. Here were none of the silk or chintz coverings to be found at Easterwood. Instead, a huge cream leather settee stood against the far wall with two matching lounger chairs. A functional pedestal desk was under the window, complete with word processor, and books and files were piled haphazardly on the floor, which was polished and uncarpeted. The fireplace was set with logs, awaiting just a match to set them blazing merrily. A long, low table stood near the bookshelves which lined one wall, and a drinks cabinet was squashed into one corner.

It was the table to which Jenny was drawn, for on it were several small wooden carvings. She moved nearer, fascinated yet conscious that this was Ben's room and she had no right to intrude. The carvings, mostly of animals, weren't Joshua's, she could see that at a glance. None was crafted with such delicacy of touch, but they had a rough-hewn charm of their own. Wondering whether they were Ben's work, she picked up an ostrich-like bird and held it aloft.

'It's meant to be a cassowary,' Ben said with a smile. 'My father inherited some of the family carving talents, though it's not as good as Joshua's work. And no, I didn't inherit any! At least——' He hesitated, then indicated the lone water-colour on the wall. 'I dabble a little—when I have the time,' he admitted self-consciously.

Now Jenny realised why there were so many paintings at the clinic. She moved to inspect this one, very much aware of Ben's presence only a few feet away. It depicted the Easterwood, painted on a stormy day with the trees bent almost double in an effort to avoid the wind, a scattering of leaves on the carriage sweep, and stick-like figures, reminiscent of Lowry, hurrying towards the open door of the Easterwood and the welcoming glow from within.

'It isn't very good, but it's meant to be symbolic, to show Easterwood welcoming people who don't feel whole, complete,' Ben explained, then went on to discuss psychiatry in general, and the clinic in particular.

They remained there long into the evening. For
Jenny, this period made up for all the trauma, all the
heartache she'd suffered. Ben lit the lamps, drew the
velvet curtains, then put on a record of Tchaikovsky's
Violin Concerto. The soothing tones of Salvatore
Accardo's violin filled the room, and Jenny closed her
eyes, relaxed at last.

'Here—a glass of wine to complement the good
music.' Her eyes fluttered open, to see Ben holding out
a glass of amber liquid which gleamed in the lamplight.

'Thank you. The perfect end to a perfect evening,'
she said quietly, thinking there were other, more
perfect ways to end such an evening. She knew she
wanted Ben to make love to her. Probably Ben knew
it, too, but. . . She sipped her wine, striving to find
some innocuous topic of conversation, but they had
pretty well exhausted the subject they had in common,
had even spoken about Stella Lawrence and her tearful
return to the ward to apologise.

'Don't you think you might have Stella back now?'
Jenny spoke into the waiting silence. She sat up,
shaking her head a little to try to clear it. She could
easily have slept in the surprisingly comfortable chair.

Ben gazed into the fire he had lit. A piece of log fell
spluttering into the hearth and he picked up the tongs
to ease it back. 'Not yet—she might do better at home.
We'll see how she gets along.'

Jenny watched the firelight playing upon his dark
features. The food and wine combined with a tired
mind and body caused her to fancy that he shimmered,
then changed into that buccaneer. She would almost
swear that a golden earring sparkled in his ear, that a
wicked-looking dagger was thrust into his belt, that
outside a winter storm raged which prevented him from
carrying her away in his ship to some savage shore
where he was king. Any moment now he would grow
impatient and, with an oath, would sweep her into his

arms and carry her up to his lair, all the while raining passionate kisses upon her eager mouth. Then, once he had laid her down on the velvet cushions he kept for seduction scenes, his strong, powerful hands would caress her, gently at first, then with increasing ardour as he sensed her response. Then—then Sister Fraser would wake up and come to her senses!

Aware that tears of laughter were streaming down her face, and aware, too, of Ben's astonished gaze, Jenny set down her glass then covered her face with her hands, her shoulders shaking. So much for erotic dreams!

'Jenny?' The pirate's voice was concerned, and she tried to control what amounted to hysteria. She shook her head numbly, then felt the pirate king take her in his arms just as she had wished. The passionate kisses didn't rain down upon her eager mouth, but this warm embrace was infinitely more comforting, and Jenny snuggled closer, her damp face pressed against his shirt.

'You're wearing a decent shirt for a change,' she said, and felt his chest heave as he chuckled.

'One of my favourite charity shop's better quality garments, I think! I'm glad you approve, Sister Jenny,' he said, his lips pressed against her ear. She knew she really ought to protest, to get up and tell him she'd had a lovely evening but she really must be going, there were some letters she simply must write. She needed to get her uniform ready for Monday night, too. Well, yes, Doctor, Saturday evening *was* rather too soon to be thinking of work on Monday night but time passed so quickly and——

She knew what she ought to do, but actually doing it was a different matter. It was difficult to concentrate on the list of weekend chores when a certain bold buccaneer's tongue was experimentally caressing her ear, when the buccaneer had, somehow, ended up sharing the same chair, when his hands were moving sensuously over her body, building up her desire to such an extent that she didn't know where she was. She was no longer capable of coherent thought, and when his hand moved down and rested on her lower abdomen she moaned aloud.

Ben's fingers splayed out and moved even lower, and Jenny's body cried out for release. 'Please, Ben,' she murmured. She wanted him to continue, to make love to her, but it wouldn't be wise. Heartbreak lay ahead. Remember Lloyd, look what *he* did to your heart. Then there was Louise. . . 'And Rachel,' she said bitterly, struggling to get up.

'I don't notice Rachel in the room,' Ben said huskily, 'but if you want me to stop, for God's sake say so! Now,' he commanded. Why did she have to mention Rachel? He couldn't see the connection, but no doubt there was one in Jenny's mind. Tentatively he brushed his lips across her brow, then began to stroke her soft hair. It smelled fragrant, newly washed, and he buried his face in it, prepared to wait until Jenny made the decision. It would hurt physically as well as emotionally to let her go, but he wasn't such a chauvinistic bastard as all that. Jenny had suffered the attentions of one; she didn't need another one.

Jenny wasn't consciously aware of making the decision, of throwing caution to the winds, but she really had no choice. Oh, yes, she knew Ben wouldn't try to coerce her. She had only to get up and he would accept her decision, but her heart gave the answer Ben wanted as she raised her face for his kiss. . .

When he gathered her up in his arms she half thought that, like the pirate king, he would take her upstairs, but instead he carried her to the settee, switched off all the lamps then knelt by her side, only the fire's glow illuminating his features. He flicked her cheek with a finger, his face expressionless. If she had hoped for words of love, they didn't come. Instead he said, 'Is this what you really want, Jenny? I care for you, I——' He stopped. 'I can't offer you undying love and devotion. I can't offer you anything at all,' he said harshly.

'Lloyd offered me his undying love. *That* I can do without,' she said, her voice scarcely audible. Then there was no more need for words as, with a tenderness Jenny wouldn't have suspected, Ben slowly undressed her, kissing her as each item of clothing was removed. Then she performed the same service for him. Or tried to, but their mutual need wouldn't wait, and they became locked in an embrace which Jenny wanted never to end.

Ben was a considerate lover, and Jenny reached new heights of ecstasy, ecstasy she wouldn't have believed possible. To give herself in love couldn't be wrong, but if only he loved her! Afterwards, she clung to him desperately, so afraid he would leave her, so afraid that reality would intrude.

In her heart she knew that, come Monday, everything would be as it was before. She would be the new night sister, he the director of the Easterwood. Here, now, it was different. They were two lost souls in a world of their own. On Monday they would be back down to planet Earth with a vengeance.

'Oh, Jenny,' Ben groaned, and Jenny pulled his head down, her arms clinging about his neck.

'Don't leave me yet,' she begged. 'Let's stay a little while longer. I could spend the night here, couldn't I?' The thought of returning to her empty flat depressed her.

Gently Ben disentangled himself, then raised himself on one elbow in the cramped space, one hand resting proprietorially on her breast. 'That wouldn't be wise, Jenny.' He kissed her lips before she could protest. 'I'll take you back now—before it's too late.'

Jenny chuckled, thinking it was already too late, but it wasn't until they made love once more that they could bear to part, Jenny believing that her own reluctance to leave his arms was more than matched by Ben's. They had given each other pleasure. In her own case, she had given with love, and she thought some of her love had reached out and touched Ben's heart. With that, she would have to be satisfied.

It was as she ran a comb through her hair that she heard the front door being opened. Her horrified gaze was mirrored by Ben's own as he glanced at his watch, then swore. 'It's after three. High time for the Rat King to take Cinderella home.' Ben's voice was bitter as he helped her to her feet, just as the sitting-room door opened and Dr Carol Smithson stood framed in the doorway, her eyes as big as saucers. As well they might be, thought Jenny, her flushed face and over-bright eyes giving away all too clearly what she had spent some considerable time doing.

'Oh, sorry, Ben! I'll be getting off to bed. Good-night!' Carol slammed the door, leaving a stunned silence behind her.

'I suppose that's why we had to make do with the settee. Carol gets first claim on the bed, does she?' Making a superhuman effort, Jenny kept her voice light, mocking. Ben might think she made a habit of this sort of thing and perhaps it was better if he did. That way he wouldn't guess how her heart was bleeding at this very moment. Let him think the episode had meant no more to her than she now realised it had to him.

If Ben, at that moment, had taken the trouble to explain Carol's presence in his house and the glaring fact that she held a key to his front door, Jenny would have listened. She was eager to hear any plausible explanation, but one wasn't offered. No excuses but no explanations, either. So Carol must have taken Louise's place. Or was it Rachel's place?

In silence Ben drove her to her flat. Jenny was coldly angry. No, not even angry, for hadn't she half expected her heart to be broken yet again? She was more stunned, disappointed, than angry. Ben was turning out to be another Lloyd Simmons. What had he called himself? Rat King. An apt title.

'Goodnight, Ben. And thank you—for everything,' she said pointedly as he stopped the car outside her flat.

'My pleasure,' he said briefly, but before he could open the car door for her she was out, forcing herself to walk calmly up to the flats even though her every instinct was to run.

She went over to the window to close the sitting-room curtains, curious to see whether Ben's car was still in the forecourt. It was. He had waited to see her safely in. Yet, if he cared about her, why hadn't he explained what Carol was doing in his house? Even as she watched, the car glided out into what remained of the night and Jenny closed the curtains tightly against the darkness, questions without answers chasing themselves across her mind.

Sunday morning she slept late, and awoke with such a headache that she decided fresh air and a change of scenery was the only cure. Sitting around moping all day wouldn't do her any good, and at the back of her mind was the thought that Ben might call on her. No, she couldn't face him. In the cool light of day she could see that there was a reasonable explanation for Carol being there. Since the girl had just moved from her last placement, she would need somewhere temporary to stay, and Ben had offered his house. Yet Carol was local, she'd said as much. She had family in Bexhill— so she wouldn't *need* to share Ben's house.

Jenny stayed out all day, taking a picnic lunch to the

seafront and sharing it with the pigeons and sparrows. When she returned to her flat in the evening, she almost expected the telephone to ring, or even to find that a note had been pushed under her door, but there was nothing.

She busied herself about the flat on Monday, then, with some trepidation, got ready to go on duty that night. She must seek Ben out the first chance she got. Sticking her head in the sand like that wooden cassowary of the Moran family wouldn't get her anywhere!

Jenny and the male staff nurse, Albert, quickly sorted out their priorities for the night. Not a great deal had happened since the previous Friday morning, except that Simon Jenkins was talking about discharging himself.

'Making wild statements about unrequited love,' Albert told her. 'I was on last night and we got talking. He's uptight about it all, won't say who the lady is,' he complained, and Jenny bit her lip, knowing only too well! But should she tell another member of staff? She decided not; that would be betraying Simon's confidence.

'He met his wife in the town last Saturday.' Her tone was non-committal. 'I gather the meeting wasn't too happy. Perhaps we could get her in one night?' she suggested, leaving it up to Albert to put the idea to the patient.

Tracking Simon down later proved difficult. When a search of the acute floor failed to produce him, Jenny thought he had found a way out and might be wandering like a lost soul somewhere. Thankfully, there appeared not to *be* a way out, but one could never be sure. Stella had confessed to Anne Bomford's involvement in her own escape. Anne had complained of feeling faint and had asked the junior porter to open the door for her to get a breath of fresh air. She had promised she wouldn't leave the clinic. And she hadn't, but while Anne distracted the young man's attention Stella had slipped out.

Then Jenny had a brainwave and made for the room at the end of the corridor. She switched on the light then waited. Simon must be there; there was nowhere else he could be. And at length a figure shambled into the light. 'Oh, hello, Sister. Sorry, is this out of bounds?'

Noting that she was 'Sister' again, Jenny gently chided him. 'You'll catch cold in here. I'll have to ask Dr Ben if we can use——'

'Yes, dear Dr Ben,' Simon said curtly. 'I expect it would be better if the room was brought into general use but then I wouldn't have anywhere to escape to, would I? It may be chilly but it has the advantage of being quiet!'

Simon avoided her eyes and she didn't try to fuss over him. The less said about his declaration of love, the better. 'I hear you want to discharge yourself. Is that wise, when you're getting on so well?' she asked as she led the way to the quiet-room.

Simon sat down, then tried to smile. 'No, I don't really want to leave, but. . .' He shrugged. 'Dr Ben isn't a bad sort, really. I had a long talk with him before he went away and he said he would get the other nurse therapist to counsel me, since I don't get on too well with Rachel.'

'Yes, that's a good idea,' Jenny agreed, startled and dismayed but trying not to show it. Ben—gone away?

The early hours of Tuesday morning produced Carol Smithson, who peered anxiously round the door at Jenny. 'Hello, not intruding, am I? I expect you don't really want doctors at night, but it's all grist to the mill,' she went on brightly, then rushed on, 'I'm sorry about Saturday night! I wanted the floor to open up and swallow me when I blundered in like that!'

'I'm afraid I jumped to the wrong conclusion and

gave Ben the sharp edge of my tongue,' Jenny admitted. 'Once I had a chance to think, I realised you were only visiting, but at the time I *couldn't* think. Has Ben. . .?' She hesitated. 'I'd like to apologise, though Ben might have said something. He didn't offer an explanation!' she went on indignantly.

'Ben's a proud man—surely you realise that? He doesn't expect to have to account for everything he does! You must have hurt him!' Carol sounded cross. 'I called at your flat on Sunday but you must have been out.'

'I spent the day by the sea,' Jenny said. 'I needed to think.'

'And now you have?'

She nodded. 'Now I have. Is Ben at home, or would it be better not to disturb him? Perhaps it's best to let sleeping dogs lie,' Jenny went on, painfully aware, as Carol was not, that Ben had said he had nothing to offer, certainly not love. Without love, what sort of relationship would it be?

Carol confirmed that Ben should be at home, though as she had moved out that morning she couldn't be sure. 'It was only for the weekend,' she explained later, as they walked the ward together. 'My family had a whole houseful and Ben offered bed and board! We've known each other for yonks, really. He doesn't see me as a woman.' The doctor sounded peeved. Another conquest for the Buccaneer, Jenny thought without rancour. Poor Ben!

Realising it was the best way, Jenny wrote a brief note to Ben and posted it as she went off duty. She had at least apologised for jumping to the wrong conclusion, and a letter saved his pride. He wouldn't have to pretend that he cared for her, that he wished their affair to continue. It allowed him an easy way out, and *she* certainly wasn't about to beg for his favours!

When next they met, she doubted if he would even

refer to the matter. The chapter was closed. If it had left Sister Fraser with a shattered heart once more, too bad. She was a survivor. Hadn't Ben himself called her 'tough as army boots'? She must prove him right.

CHAPTER THIRTEEN

JENNY was glad to go off duty on Friday morning. She had, by now, convinced herself that she cared nothing for Ben. But, since she hadn't seen him for almost a week, she wasn't able to put this new-found conviction to the test.

Then, too, the altercation with Anne Bomford had left her drained. She had tried to reason with the girl, pointing out that if Anne herself had special privileges, others would expect them, too. Perhaps a newcomer might take advantage of being let into the grounds at night, might even attack one of the old folk downstairs. This last argument seemed to impress Anne, who loved old people, but one could never be sure how much had taken root. Time would tell.

Ben's car drew up as she walked out to her own, and Jenny's heart started its painful fluttering. Here he was at last, just as she had wished, and she didn't know what to say to him.

'You might say, "Good morning, Doctor,"' Ben suggested unsmilingly, as he stood, hands in pockets.

'Good morning, Doctor,' Jenny intoned. 'I'm sorry—for going on like that on Saturday. I should have realised——' She broke off.

'I'm sorry for not explaining, but I didn't see the need.'

No, of course he wouldn't. Jenny was only the night nurse; there was no need to explain to *her*! Her expression was as cool as his own, then he disconcerted her by chuckling.

'You're looking frosty, Sister Jenny. Did somebody

171

annoy you?' Ben enquired mildly, laughter lurking in
the dark depths of his eyes.

'No—why ever should you think that, Doctor? No
one ever annoys me!'

'Perhaps we should begin again?' Ben suggested.

'Begin *what* again?' They traded glances, Jenny
coldly furious, Ben calm and unperturbed. Silence
reigned for a moment or two, then she dropped her
gaze to her clenched hands. Why didn't he leave her in
peace? 'You don't give me any peace!' she spoke into
the silence, and Ben looked startled.

'You don't give *me* any peace. I'm beginning to wish
you hadn't come to Easterwood,' he said bluntly, and
Jenny gasped, two spots of colour burning her cheeks.

'You can have my notice tomorrow, Dr Moran! At
least we know where we stand now! I——' No—she
wouldn't be chased away like that! 'On second
thoughts, I withdraw my resignation.' She eyed him
defiantly.

'Oh? Why is that, Sister?' They were within touching
distance now, and he reached out and clasped both her
hands in his. 'Tell me, and if your reason is a sensible
one, I'll consider letting you keep your job.'

'Ben, please. . . People can see us!' Jenny tugged
unavailingly. Ben held on to her hands as though he
never meant to let go.

'I need to talk to you, Jenny, and not about patients.
Forget them for a few minutes—OK?'

She glanced down despairingly at their clasped
hands, then nodded. 'If you wish. Though I can't see
what we have to discuss if we don't talk about the
patients. That's why we're both here, after all.'

'We have a hell of a lot to discuss, and you know it!'
For once, Ben had lost his cool, and Jenny's eyes
widened.

'Shame on you, Dr Ben. You're supposed to be
even-tempered, equable, kind, soothing——'

'Generous to a fault, wimpish,' Ben finished for her, and laughter bubbled up inside her.

'No—o,' she spluttered, 'I'd rather you weren't wimpish! But really, Ben, we haven't anything to discuss. Saturday night and Sunday morning was Saturday night and Sunday morning,' she said quietly. 'This is Friday morning—a whole world away.' She forced herself to look into his eyes, but long, coal-black lashes hid his expression from her.

'It isn't a whole world away to me, Jenny,' he said softly. 'I——' He so very nearly said, 'I love you,' but bit back the words in time. It was too soon. Always a determined man who swept obstacles aside and feared nothing, Ben now found himself facing an obstacle he couldn't surmount. If only he could be sure Jenny loved him! No, she was still pining for that guy and it would be love on the rebound—a dangerous thing. He must be patient, woo her gently, help her to put the past behind her. Anyway, after Louise, he intended treading cautiously himself. Reining in his ardour wasn't easy, but years of training told. He, too, glanced down at their hands, then gently released her.

Somehow he withstood the temptation to run his fingers through her smooth, silky hair. Instead he said, 'I've promised that dog another run—will you join me? That's an order, by the way,' he said, as she hesitated.

'It's the end of my nights,' Jenny said warily. Walking the dog might lead to other, more interesting events. 'I'll be too tired—but I'll think of you and Suki,' she promised.

'I'll pick you up from your flat after you've had a chance to wash and change,' Ben said, his tone brooking no refusal. 'Fresh air and exercise is just what the doctor ordered. Take care.' Then he was gone, and she was left staring at her car, her thoughts troubled.

Yes, by all means I'll help you walk the dog, Dr Ben, she mused, but what about Rachel? She had

taken a back seat since the arrival of the glamorous
Carol Smithson, and if Jenny was any judge the woman
was heading for a complete breakdown. If Ben cared
about that, he certainly didn't show his feelings. Once
before, Jenny had thought it a pity that there was no
one to listen to the problems of the nursing staff. They
had a high turnover of patients, presumably all part of
the 'results and quota' system Fay Whalley had once
spoken about. That placed greater pressure on staff.
Jenny tilted her determined chin. Ben might end up
regretting he'd asked her for walkies!

Suki remembered her from last Saturday, and it was
some moments before Jenny could greet Ben properly.
Be friendly, she told herself, but not over-friendly.
Make sure he doesn't get the wrong idea!

'We won't walk far, Jenny. You must be tired.' Ben's
voice was strained, and Jenny gave him a searching
look.

'You look as tired as I feel,' she countered, 'but I'm
afraid I've got lots of problems for you to solve!'

'Good. Let's hear them.' Ben offered his arm as they
strolled through the parkland towards the village. His
nearness was disconcerting. If only he cared as she did!
Even if she told him she loved him, what then? He
would stand there, outwardly calm, trying to find words
to tell her she had no hopes in that direction. Oh, he
would be kind, considerate of her feelings, but no,
however kindly worded, was still no.

'Jenny?' he prompted, and, keeping her eyes fixed
on the dog, she poured out her thoughts about an
occupational health nurse. It was something she had
voiced before, and Ben had promised they would put
it to a staff meeting, but now, seeing how wretched
Rachel looked, Jenny thought the matter more urgent.
Of course, if Ben returned Rachel's love, she probably
wouldn't look wretched, but she must try to persuade

Ben that an occupational health nurse or a nurse-counsellor would be for the good of all the staff.

'I've thought about that before,' Ben commented, as they reached the end of the park. Whistling to the dog, he clipped the lead on again, but instead of heading for the village he led Jenny towards a twitten. 'This will bypass the village,' he explained. 'After this, there's another little path leading to the common pond. It's peaceful there.'

Before they reached the common pond, Ben returned Suki to her owner, an elderly disabled lady. 'Suki's had a good walk,' he commented. 'Louise used to visit her owner every now and again,' he went on slowly.

'Whenever she got the impulse?' Jenny suggested, and Ben frowned down at her.

'Clever of you to work that out. Louise was a creature of impulse—very Aries! So kind-hearted you wouldn't believe it, but. . .'

Jenny waited, aware that Ben didn't really want to talk about his wife, but that he needed to, none the less: one-to-one therapy for the psychiatrist.

'We were both in our thirties when we married,' Ben said quietly. 'I guess we were too independent to share a proper home life. Neither of us would compromise, meet the other one halfway. By then, I'd had enough of roaming the world, but Louise was bored with England. She wanted glamour, excitement. Yet we had some good times. She was well-liked, good to animals and the handicapped. We were just incompatible and ended up leading two separate lives.' He sounded in pain but Jenny deemed it wiser not to offer words of comfort.

They stared down at the murky pond in silence before Ben continued, 'Louise said she was attracted to my good looks! Perhaps I was attracted to hers.' He wondered if that was all it had been—a superficial relationship based on beauty rather than trust and mutual affection. 'It's only five months since she died, but I'd be a liar if I said I missed her.' He glanced over at Jenny. 'Does that shock you?'

'No. Apart from the den, there was no life in your house,' she mused. 'The sitting-room was empty, devoid of anyone's personality.'

'Louise's personality came to life when she was away from home and in the limelight. Maybe Dean Bonner was able to give her what I couldn't—unstinting admiration. And time. I was always too busy. I hope she was happy with him. She deserved it,' Ben said softly, thinking that this lady by his side deserved happiness more than Louise.

There was a cool breeze playing across the deserted pond, and after a few moments they strolled on, arm in arm. To get Ben's thoughts away from the hurtful past, Jenny said, 'Will you bring up the question of the nurse-counsellor before the meeting?'

'Will do. I mentioned it to Shirley Ross once and we had quite an argument about it. She was kind of extrovert. She thought we could all discuss our personal problems in a staff meeting—group therapy,' Ben said with a wry smile.

'That I would like to see! Dr Les complaining about his children, Rachel complaining about hers, you——' Jenny paused, before going on, 'You complaining because everyone else was moaning! I could tell them about Lloyd, couldn't I?' She strived to keep her tone light, playful, but doubted if she deceived Ben.

'Do you think about him much?' he wanted to know, and she tensed. If she said she didn't, Ben might think that left the field free for him. No! She mustn't let him think she was over Lloyd, ready for another love-affair.

'Yes, I do. Quite a lot,' she said instead.

'That's perfectly natural,' was Ben's only comment. Yet, for them both, the magic was gone from the day.

As they skirted the pond and retraced their steps, he said, 'Life's too short to waste, Jenny. Take my advice and put the past behind you, reach out for the future. I'm good at handing out advice but I never take it myself,' he said with a faint smile.

'Then you shouldn't waste any more time,' she said decisively, stopping in her tracks. She turned to face him, trying to hide the anguish she felt, but she would be less than just to Rachel if she said nothing. Perhaps Rachel could give Ben what he needed—a real home, a ready-made family. Perhaps, later, there would be children of his own. . . Taking a deep breath, she said, 'Rachel needs you, Ben! Can't you see that? She's getting more wretched by the day. You said she had to come to terms with it, but she can't. She feels——' Jenny hesitated, not wanting to say that Rachel believed her to be a rival. 'She needs support and help. As mental health workers, we ought to offer that support,' she finished lamely.

'That wasn't what you were going to say. Don't tell me Rachel's jealous of you?'

'I know the idea is ridiculous,' Jenny said tightly. Ben didn't need to make his astonishment quite so obvious. 'When people are worried, they tend to magnify every little problem, every slight. They——'

'Thank you, Sister, I *have* had some experience of psychiatry,' Ben said drily.

Feeling foolish, Jenny tried again. 'Rachel loves you! Surely you can see your attitude is making her unhappy. . .?' Her voice trailed away. She didn't want to mention the unofficial engagement Rachel had spoken about. She was beginning to realise, too late, that it had been a figment of the therapist's imagination.

'I can't pretend to love her, Jenny. I told you there was nothing between us and that's God's own truth! Rachel loved Dean, despite everything. If she's pining away, it's for him, not me.' Ben's tone was dismissive. 'Shirley Ross was one of Dean's lovers, but that was before he met Louise. You're not to take on Rachel's troubles, honey. She can look after herself,' he warned.

Jenny looked at him, her eyes wondering. He had called her 'honey'! 'That's another Americanism. What happened to your Greek and Australian heritage?' she asked laughingly, not wanting him to realise how pleased she was.

Ben chuckled as they emerged once more into the lane. 'I told you, I'm a citizen of the world.' He hesitated briefly, then went on, 'I was in Vietnam. I made some good friends out there, of all nationalities.'

'You fought in the war?' Jenny was startled. Although she'd thought, right at the beginning, that he looked tough enough to take care of himself anywhere, she couldn't imagine the tolerant, equable Ben Moran actually fighting, killing. . .

He nodded curtly. 'I was young then, adventurous, idealistic. It was only later that I began planning a different kind of life. I took up medicine and I'm glad I did. I've seen so much bloodshed that I opt for a quiet existence these days. Can you understand that?'

'Of course,' she murmured. 'Did—is that why you limp a little? I shouldn't mention it,' she rushed on, 'but someone said it was an old war wound.'

'That's a legacy of Beirut. I was under siege there for a few days once.' He laughed shortly, the memories unpleasant. 'I was out there visiting a colleague I'd trained with. She was killed,' he said bluntly, 'and I survived.'

Jenny listened with a growing sense of horror. Ben had been through all that, yet could still care about others. There was more to the Buccaneer than met the eye and only now was she beginning to realise it, to know the real Ben. How weak and foolish and small her own troubles seemed.

Mistaking her silence for reproach, Ben clammed up. Idly Jenny twisted off a leaf as they passed a hedgerow, then shredded it carefully as she thought before speaking. Whatever happened, she mustn't hurt him more. 'I'm glad you told me that,' she said at last. 'I always thought you looked tough and capable,' she went on with a glimmer of a smile. 'Now I know! You must have nine lives!'

'If I have, I've still plenty of them left,' Ben assured her, a warm smile lighting up his features. He reached for her hand, deciding it was make or break time. 'When you're over that guy, remember I'm here. OK?'

Startled, Jenny looked at him. Then, where they could be seen by passers-by, Ben kissed her swiftly, the kiss searing her lips, leaving her shaken as never before.

'Ben, I——' she began, but he shook his head at her.

'Don't say anything now, just remember that Ben the Buccaneer's still around.'

Just *what* was Ben proposing? she wondered. Not marriage, that much was certain, and she couldn't face the uncertainties of another affair. She licked her suddenly dry lips, not knowing what to say. She needed time to think. No more split-second decisions where her life was concerned!

They were soon back at her flat, but Ben declined her hesitant invitation to lunch. 'How about dinner at the Artful Pheasant tomorrow night, though?' he suggested. 'There's a lot I want to say to you.' He smiled at her, that slow, heart-warming smile she had grown to love, but she had to watch it fade as she shook her head.

'I can't, Ben. I wish I could,' she admitted. 'One of my friends is coming from Glasgow. She's nursing up there and we're meeting in London—she knows someone who will put us up for the weekend. She's marrying

and going to live in Canada, so I really can't let her
down. But I'd love to come another time,' she assured
him, wanting him to know it wasn't an excuse.

Ben shrugged. 'I'll find plenty to do at Easterwood.
You enjoy your weekend, Jenny. It will give you time
to think,' he added meaningfully.

Jenny swallowed nervously, wishing they could be
alone, wishing. . . But she'd spent her life wishing.
This was for real! She stood on tiptoe and brushed her
lips against his. 'I'll ring you when I get back.'

Her eyes tried to tell him what her tongue could not,
as yet, say, but that enigmatic smile was back on his
face, and with Ben it was difficult to know what he was
thinking. The professional mask was there too often
for her liking. Well, she would strip it from him, piece
by piece. If Rachel needed someone to confide in, Ben
needed one even more! And, from next week, *she* was
going to be his confidante, no matter that he couldn't
offer her marriage, or even love. Pride was a cold
bedfellow. She couldn't remember where she had read
that, but it was true. Her good resolution about weigh-
ing up the pros and cons before plunging into another
love-affair vanished as if it had never been, but Ben
was right—she needed to get away from Easterwood
for a while.

They kissed briefly before she ran indoors, making
light work of the three flights of stairs today, and
feeling that she wanted to burst into song. When she
returned on Monday morning, she would ring Ben
straight away.

She was destined not to spend the whole weekend
with her friend, for that evening, just as she was
packing for an early start, she had a visitor: Lloyd
Simmons. At the insistent ringing of the doorbell, she
thought immediately of Ben, and was less than pleased
to see her stepfather there. If her greeting lacked

welcome, Lloyd appeared not to notice. There was an air of strain about him she hadn't seen before.

'You look as if you need something sustaining, Lloyd. How about a whisky?' Since she drank nothing stronger than wine, Lloyd's eyebrows shot up, and she flushed, not wanting him to know she'd bought a bottle especially for a certain pirate king of her acquaintance!

'Hitting the hard stuff already, love? It's just what I need. Thanks.' Without being invited, Lloyd threw himself down on the armchair, then, with a frown, he glanced at the weekend case parked on the settee. 'Not leaving, are you? Jen?' There was uncertainty in his voice but she saw no reason to enlighten him.

'What can I do for you? You didn't come down just to drink my best Scotch.'

'I doubt if it's yours. A little sparkling wine is more your taste, Jen. Whose is it? Will he mind?'

She wouldn't be drawn. 'Perhaps my tastes have changed. In all things,' she added, and Lloyd shrugged. 'How is my mother?' she asked after a moment.

'She isn't too grand. She's got to go in for an operation—something to do with her ovaries. Oh, I don't understand these things,' he rushed on. 'I thought you might come up with me and see her.' When Jenny met his request with a stony silence, he rushed on, 'It wasn't Angie's idea, Jen, it was mine. She doesn't know I'm here. I know we treated you badly, but we——'

'Yes, you did.' With an effort, Jenny kept her voice steady, remembering as she did so the anguish as she'd opened that envelope, read the cutting announcing their marriage. 'You hurt me. Both of you. That's something I can't forgive—or forget. But bitterness corrodes and revenge isn't sweet. I know that now. I don't want revenge—I just want to be left in peace.'

With a sigh, Lloyd got up, replacing his glass on the occasional table and leaving a damp mark. Typical, she thought. Ben wouldn't do that. He. . . 'If Angie wants to see me, then I'll come,' she said, surprising herself. She loved Ben, that courageous, caring man, and she knew *he* would wish her to go.

Still wondering whether she was doing the right thing, she got into Lloyd's car later that evening, but once again her plans were changed, this time because Lloyd nearly hit a pedestrian as they swept through the village. He was busily accelerating as they approached a zebra crossing and didn't heed Jenny's warning.

He stopped abruptly as Jenny snapped, 'You fool! I have to go back and see if that woman's all right.'

'I didn't knock her down, for heaven's sake!' he snapped back, but Jenny was already out of the car and running back to see if first aid was needed. Someone else was there before her—Rachel Bonner!

'Your friend's in an almighty hurry,' Rachel said sourly, as they made sure the pedestrian hadn't come to harm. With angry remarks about 'maniacs who should be locked up', the woman hurried away, leaving Rachel obviously wondering about the expensive car—and the handsome man.

'Yes, we have to get to London. I'm spending the weekend there,' Jenny admitted. She was in half a mind to ask Rachel to tell Ben her plans had been changed, but that would have been cruel. Ben would have to tell the woman himself about their relationship. She had tried to ring him several times at his home, and she supposed he must be at the clinic. She would phone him when they got to London.

Again, there was no reply when she tried his home number and a weary and dispirited Jenny didn't want to phone him at the Easterwood.

Feeling the Fates were conspiring to thwart her at every turn, she paid a brief and painful visit to her mother the following day. They cried together, becoming closer in so doing than they had ever been before.

If Ben could have been there with her, the weekend would have been perfect, but Monday would soon come, she told herself.

'Thank you for coming,' Angie said simply, as Jenny saw her into the hospital on Monday morning and prepared to take a train home—home to Easterwood and to Ben. 'Say a prayer for me! That's a laugh, isn't it? Still, take care, Jenny, love.'

Rembering the little church, Jenny knew she would say that prayer, and mean it.

On Monday afternoon she tried to sleep but could not. Her brain was whirling with new sensations, and always there was Ben. She had meant to bring him something from London, a little offering to show she had missed him, but Angie had taken up too much time. Then, too, there had been an all too brief meeting with her friend. All she had managed was a cheap gift from a shop near the station—a gaudy green and red striped scarf which she decided was just the thing for a pirate to wear at the talent night! He would make a magnificent swashbuckler. And she would go as the swashbuckler's moll! *That* would give the patients a laugh!

Abandoning the idea of much-needed sleep, Jenny tried to ring Ben again, and eventually found him at the clinic. He was, she was told, in a meeting with Rachel Bonner but would be given the message as soon as he was free.

There was no reason why he shouldn't be having a meeting. No reason, either, why Rachel shouldn't be there, yet it was Rachel who had seen her in Lloyd's car. She nibbled her lower lip thoughtfully, then shrugged away the unease—unease that increased by the hour as time slipped away and still Ben didn't phone. He had probably decided not to bother. He would be on the ward tonight, anyway. Yes, she would see him then.

But it was a weary, sad-eyed night sister who drove to the clinic that evening. She felt all her problems crowding back in on her. Surely if Ben still cared, was still of the same mind, he would have made time to contact her, if only for a few seconds? The meeting couldn't have taken hours!

Yet she was her usual cheerful self as she listened to the hand-over a short while later. She and Resi would be sharing the honours tonight and she longed to ask her colleague whether Ben was coming on duty, but restrained herself. No, she told herself, she would be practical over *this* romance. She wouldn't wear her heart on her sleeve this time—men took unfair advantage of women like that.

'So, what's new?' she asked instead.

'Simon and Ben are building up a good rapport,' Resi said, eyeing her. 'You can see the notes for yourself, but he admitted to Ben that he often loitered in the corridor outside this office—your office—hoping to catch a glimpse of you.'

'It must have taken courage to admit that,' Jenny acknowledged. 'But I'm glad he did. I've sometimes felt myself watched when I've been in the corridor. It's reassuring to know it wasn't due to my over-active imagination!'

Resi nodded. 'I think he's well on the way to recovery. Once the symptoms subside Ben's going to discharge him. Anne is to be seen by the psychologist and Ben thinks he may have a placement for her soon.'

Ben again. It seemed to Jenny that Resi's every sentence was about Ben. Of course that was nonsense, but later, when she was alone, Jenny wasn't surprised to see the man herself. The smile of welcome died on her lips as she saw him standing just outside the office door. His eyes were bleak, his lips compressed and his jaw rigid as he surveyed her. 'Ben?' she said uncertainly. 'What is it?'

'When I heard you were spending the weekend with Lloyd Simmons, I thought, Another Louise,' Ben said conversationally. 'Can you imagine that?' He came into the room and slumped down in the chair in front of her.

'You thought I was another Louise?' Jenny said faintly, seating herself carefully behind the desk, anxious to keep that barrier between them. 'Did I spend the weekend with Lloyd?' She tilted her proud head, waiting. She wasn't going to apologise, to hurry with an explanation. If he didn't trust her now, he never would. But *you* didn't trust him when you found Carol there, did you? a nasty little voice chuckled in her ear, and she went rosy, something Ben couldn't fail to notice. She saw his eyes narrow, and that bleakness was still there.

'I don't know, quite honestly,' Ben admitted, then leaned forward. 'But if I ever catch you being unfaithful when we're married, I'll make you wish you'd never been born. Caesar's wife is supposed to be above reproach. Louise wasn't, but. . .' He paused. 'I don't want to think of you in some other guy's bed. I couldn't take that,' he said gruffly.

A warm glow of happiness lit Jenny's eyes. Then Ben went on. 'What were you doing with that guy, anyway? Has something happened to your mother?'

'Mm, Angie's going to have an operation—a hysterectomy. Lloyd came down and asked me to call on her. I thought about refusing but she's still my mother.' Ben nodded, his eyes never leaving her face. 'What was that about being married?' she went on, folding her arms. '*I* don't remember being asked.'

'I'm not asking you, I'm telling you. Who's in charge of this place, anyway? That's an order, Sister Fraser!'

'I'm not sure I want to marry you, doctor's orders or no doctor's orders! You're domineering, bossy——' She began to tick off his faults on her fingers. 'What else? Ah, yes, arrogant, authoritarian, obviously addicted to dogs and to working twenty-four hours a day. Now that is something I couldn't accept, Dr Moran.'

'The dogs or the twenty-four-hour day?' Ben got up and placed his large, capable hands on the desk in front of her. 'I'd kinda like to kiss you, but I'm sure there's an Easterwood rule against that kind of thing. Still, rules were made to be broken, weren't they?' He leant forward, his lips caressing her cheeks, her neck, her hair, and knocking her lace cap sideways.

'Really, Doctor,' she remonstrated with him. 'I can't have that sort of behaviour on *my* ward! Oh—what about Resi? I've left her to do all the work and——'

Another kiss silenced her, and the lace cap finally gave up the struggle and slid to the floor. 'I've bribed Resi to keep the ward running smoothly while I sort out a few problems with the adorable Sister Fraser,' he murmured against her ear, then there was no more need for words.

It was a flushed and happy Jenny who pulled herself out of his arms a while later, then dived into her tote bag, triumphantly producing a small package. 'I bought this for you in London, Ben. Angie didn't leave me much time to myself, so it isn't anything, really, but when I saw it I thought of you.'

Ben stared in amazement as she deftly tied the gaudy scarf around his head. Since he was dressed in dark jeans and an open-necked black shirt, her imagination was able to supply the golden earring. Then she saw that the gold was for real: he was wearing a delicate double chain around his neck, perhaps an identity necklet.

'It's for the talent night,' she whispered, as she was once more engulfed in his embrace. 'I thought we might go as Ben the Buccaneer and his moll!'

'That's the best idea you've had in nights, Sister

Fraser,' he said. Then he unfastened the clasp of the chain and held it out to her. 'This is for the night sister. It's an old Australian custom I just invented. The giver gets to wear the necklace first, then presents it to his beloved. You can't wear it while you're in uniform, Sister, so I'll give it to you when I've undressed you, shall I?'

'Dr Ben!' Jenny's tone was scandalised, as, once more, their lips met.

Talent night was a resounding success, with most of the patients managing to contribute something. Peggy danced energetically across the ballroom, Simon recited some poetry he'd written himself. The poem entitled 'To a Fair Lady' might have been aimed at Jenny, but she pretended not to realise that. Anne proved to have a strong if not entirely tuneful singing voice, and had even persuaded Sophie to dance, a mesmerising butterfly dance which earned the girl thunderous applause.

Dr Forster whistled a selection from *West Side Story*, but the climax was the fancy-dress parade, and Jenny and the rest of the night staff had spent hours helping to sew costumes. A certain consultant psychiatrist brought the house down as 'Ben the Buccaneer', so did the new night sister who, asserting her independence, decided to appear separately, as Nell Gwynn. Since she didn't have the bosomy attributes of that lady, Jenny found herself having to do rather a lot of padding, but the oranges were real enough!

The best part of the evening came later, when psychiatrist and sister shared that leather settee in Ben's den. This time no one came to disturb them, and, much later, they even found time to talk. It was almost dawn by then, Sunday morning, and they lay together and watched the sky lighten imperceptibly.

Ben's hand trailed gently down her body, coming to

rest on her flat abdomen. 'Penny for your thoughts,
Sister Fraser?' he murmured, with that lazy smile she
loved so much.

'I was thinking that Les Arifuddin must be chief
guest at the wedding. He said I was just what you
needed. Do you remember?'

'So he did. He deserves a raise! He knew what I
needed better than I did myself. That's why he interviewed you himself, without Fay Whalley. Did you
know that? *She* chose Sister Ross and lived to regret it.
They both had laid-back ideas, but patients need to
know where the line is drawn, just as staff do. I guess
we're all institutionalised! You told me the nurses were
wary of you at first. After Shirley, they didn't know
what to expect. A stern disciplinarian, probably.' Ben
rolled over on to his back, taking Jenny with him, but
she prised herself out of his grasp and got up.

'There's just one thing I *would* like to ask you,
Doctor, dear,' she said, kneeling by his side. 'That first
day I arrived. Someone phoned you at the clinic and
you said you wouldn't be home till six.' Gently she
tugged at one of the dark hairs on his chest, and he
imprisoned her hand, beginning to stroke it.

'And?' he prompted.

'I want to know who it was. If I have a rival tucked
away somewhere, I intend to challenge her to unarmed
combat!'

Ben's deep-throated chuckle warmed her. 'Jealous
already, *agapimeni*? I recall I did have a friend visiting
about then. Even psychiatrists are human. Which
reminds me,' he said, reaching for her again.

'No—I fancy a nice cup of tea, Dr Ben. Oh, and I
wanted to show you an article in the local—I meant to
show you yesterday. There's a Martello tower for sale
just up the coast and I thought——'

Jenny wasn't allowed to finish, and what she thought
quickly became submerged in what they both wanted.

BARBARY WHARF

Will Gina Tyrrell succeed in her plans to oust
Nick Caspian from the Sentinel –
or will Nick fight back?

There is only one way for Nick to win, but it might,
in the end, cost him everything!

The final book in the Barbary Wharf series

SURRENDER

Available from November 1992   Price: £2.99

W⊕RLDWIDE

— MEDICAL ROMANCE —

The books for enjoyment this month are:

A PERFECT HERO Caroline Anderson
THE HEALING HEART Marion Lennox
DOCTOR'S TEMPTATION Sonia Deane
TOMORROW IS ANOTHER DAY Hazel Fisher

♥ ♥ ♥ ♥ ♥

Treats in store!

Watch next month for the following absorbing stories:

BEYOND HEAVEN AND EARTH Sara Burton
SISTER AT HILLSIDE Clare Lavenham
IN SAFE HANDS Margaret O'Neill
STORM IN PARADISE Judith Worthy